FORESIGHT

Printed in Australia

Shawline Publishing Group Pty Ltd
www.shawlinepublishing.com.au

Paperback ISBN- 9781922751461

Ebook ISBN- 9781922751546

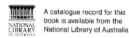 A catalogue record for this
book is available from the
National Library of Australia

FORESIGHT

CRAIG FORD

IN THE BEGINNING

LIFE IS FUNNY, ISN'T IT? You think you know what you have in store but then something happens and it changes everything. Sometimes for good, sometimes for the worse but it's those moments that seem to just happen in front of our eyes without us even noticing or acknowledging the occurrence but the impact of these events are far reaching and can change the entire direction we were working towards. I have had several of these moments in my life, but none more prevalent in my mind than losing my mother.

There was no gruesome murder or horrible car crash or anything along those lines. My mother just woke up one day and decided that she didn't want to live the suburban lifestyle anymore. She didn't want to give up her youth being a mother. She was only 18 years old when she had me. My parents were quite young when I decided to grace the world with my beloved charm and throw their plans to the wayside. Yes, I am almost one hundred percent certain that I, 'Samantha Erkhart' was a mistake, surprise, nightmare, and so totally unplanned. My parents were almost finished high school when Jenny (my mother) found out that she was expecting a child. She cried for days when she found out, if you are to believe what my grandparents told me.

Jenny had plans, finish high school, go to university and then travel Europe for six or more months before coming back to make it as a big-time lawyer or accountant or whatever it was that she thought was more important than being a mother to me. I don't remember her much I was only two when she left, I just know she was very pretty from the pictures I have seen of her. My grandparents occasionally pull some out for me to look at but I assume she has lost some of that beauty by now, 15 years have passed since she walked out on us. I hope the years haven't been kind to her and they have taken their toll. I hope she failed at achieving the glorious life she walked out on us to create. I hope what she did to me haunts her every day but I bet she doesn't lose one ounce of sleep and never has. Jenny is a self-centred bitch, and I doubt she even cares about how I turned out all these years later.

I think it's pretty obvious that I am not a big fan of my mother. I'm a little bitter and resentful. I think it is part of my charm. The whole moody teenager fits perfect for my stereotypical upbringing, don't you think? I've had a pretty good life with my dad though, I honestly have and I think we have been better off without Jenny. I know my dad misses her sometimes. Surprisingly, he still loves her and never says a bad thing about her. If I were him, I would trash talk her till the cows come home—she left us with not a second thought so why should we give her any kind of respect.

He has never gone on any dates or even really looked at another woman since she left which is a little sad, but when I have talked with him over the last few years about putting himself out there, he always just says that he has everything he needs with the two of us. I love it when he says that, but I would never admit that to him. Maybe I should though.

Dad works in construction and has done for as long as I remember. These days he manages builds of big skyscrapers and they keep him very busy. So busy that we don't see much of each other during the week, but he always comes and says hello when he gets home at night. I love my dad. He has always made sure I was looked after and I know on a few occasions he went without a lot of things to ensure I had a roof over my head, clothed and was fed well. I hit the jackpot on the dad front, that's something I know for sure.

Dad not being around though has allowed me to get entangled in a world he wouldn't even understand or probably approve of. A world of deceit, manipulation and a lot of filth if you knew where to look for it. I am a hacker. Yes, a hacker. I laugh when I see the depiction of a hacker in news or media. They are mostly men in dark-coloured hoodies with this weird background of 'matrix' code streaming down the screens. Honestly, many of the best hackers in the world are girls just like me.

I look more like a typical girl next door than what everyone thinks a hacker looks like. That misconception, has its advantages for me. Who would expect the girl next door? No one, right? They believe that I would be more likely to be out getting my nails done, than to be able to hack into your car's autopilot system. Recently, I saw a couple of guys win a new tesla for just pointing out basic issues in the cars operating system that could allow them to manipulate the cars heating and cooling. It would be funny to turn on the cooling in a car, to make it as cold as Antarctica or maybe even as hot as a sauna but it's not really that big of a deal. Not one that is worth winning a free car for anyway.

I wasn't sure if I should tell them I could take full control of the car without interaction from the occupants. I did that to our neighbour's car just for fun. He's a perv. I see him looking at me all the time and I just wanted to have some fun with him, maybe teach him a bit of a lesson. He doesn't know about that though, and I should probably try to keep it that way. If only he knew. Makes me smile just the thought of how safe people think their electronic devices are. I think many would lose a lot of sleep if they knew what some of us can do.

People have no idea that hackers are just normal people. You probably know some of them but you just don't know it—they are probably right in front of you. I have been one of them for three or four years now, maybe longer. If I really think about it, I have probably been one all my life. I have always just had this natural ability, almost like machines talk to me. When I have a target, I kind of just focus and I can see what I need to do. It sort of visualises for me in my mind's eye or something. I know, right? It sounds crazy just thinking about it, but it's a gift that has made me the perfect hacker.

I have done some things to become part of the community in the underground scene where I am known as 'Foresight'. I know it's a bit corny, but I visualise my attacks and I came up with the handle when I was like thirteen or fourteen years old. It was about then when I started to poke around the deep web. I always heard of this dark festering cesspool of a place called the dark web and I wanted to know more, but mostly it's pretty tame. It's just a bunch of old conspiracy dudes not wanting their governments to see what they do online. Oh and then there are the usual terrorists or criminals selling everything from your baggie of marijuana to warheads. It is a place you can buy whatever you want, no questions asked, as long as you have enough bitcoin to pay for it.

My normal world is pretty average, although I don't know if the world everyone sees is my real world, or if the life I hide in cyberspace is my truest self. However, let's just say for simplicity's sake, that the life lived by 17-year-old high school student Sam, is my normal world. I am a normal 17-year-old girl. I want what anyone wants, to get through high school reasonably unscathed. I am not one of those popular girls or one that is popular with the boys for all the wrong reasons. I just go to school, do my work and just let it pass me by, just kind of watching it all from a distance.

I have my friends and school isn't that bad, but there is nothing extraordinary about this existence. Yeah, I am reasonably pretty and I get noticed by the boys on occasion, but that doesn't fascinate me. I shut down any sort of advances, I just want to finish my time here and move on to university. I want to break the girl next door image and become something else. I am not sure exactly what that something else is just yet, but there has to be more than just this for me in my life.

I need to get out of my head and finish my homework before dad gets home. It's Friday and we always have dinner together in front of the TV. We always watch some sort of new movie together; we don't have a particular genre or anything. Dad just chooses one at the DVD store on the way home from work and gets us a burger and fries from the takeaway store next door. I know what you are thinking, who still watches DVDs? No one, right. It would be so much easier if we just used Netflix or something like everyone else these days but its Dad's thing and I like to just go with it. We are probably one of the few customers the store has left. I could probably get all of the movies for free, but I don't have the heart to tell my dad that. It's our thing and I like it.

It's strange how little things like that matter, isn't it? The time we spend together each week means more to me than anything else in my life. I think it does to my dad as well, but I don't think it would be something he would admit though. It would be a little too mushy for his liking. I hear his truck pull up in the garage and it puts a smile on my face, one of those real smiles that comes from the inside not one of those fake ones many of us put on when we greet someone on the street or something like that. I wonder what corny movie he has chosen for us today. I hope he didn't forget about the extra salt on my chips.

I close the lid of my laptop and make my way down the hallway. My dad is unpacking the takeaway and setting it out on plates for us to go sit in the lounge room together. As I pick up my plate, I see he has opted for a classic movie choice tonight, and one of my favourites: *The Matrix*. It's no surprise really when you think about it that Neo would be an idol of mine; it's a wonder I didn't make my hacker handle Neo. That would probably have been too much though.

AFTER SCHOOL ACTIVITIES

⊡

LIKE MANY TEENAGERS, school is not my thing. Don't get me wrong I don't hate school or anything, but it just goes by as a sort of daydream that I am taking part in but don't engage with. It just happens and I go with it. Like the flow of a gentle river, it just turns and dips, just going in the direction it is encouraged to go but it doesn't interact or respond it just flows. I do as required, interact as little as possible and just wait. Wait until the day ends and I can re-enter what feels like my true reality. Cyberspace, the internet on all levels, not just the ones most see but the deep dark corners where the boogie man would hide all his secrets.

I feel really at home as Foresight, my alter ego of sorts. She isn't like me though; she's ruthless, unforgiving and is a respected member of the hacking world. Maybe even feared a little if I am being honest. I have been working on a project of sorts the last few weeks that is bigger than I have ever done before, it will concrete my place in the cyber world if anyone ever found out it was me but it is risky and I need to make sure that I am taking the proper precautions. It's not going to be easy.

I have already gained access to all of the primary sites the marketplace is hosted from and have escalated my permissions. My payload has trickled down through into all corners of their network. Every machine in every location has my agent on it. It was a bit of a labour of love, the agent. It has been created to shut out all other interactions or commands and only accept mine. It has a self-destruct component that if I do not send a pulse within 24 hours after the assault starts, it will start an erasure protocol and hide my tracks for me. Although I have been careful and cleaned my tracks as I moved through the systems. Ensuring that I only clear my logs and my activities. All others remain intact.

I know what you are thinking. if I created an erasure protocol in my agent, then why clean my tracks as I went? Simple, if my agent is found, I don't want it to come back to me in any way, not just for my safety but for dad's as well. These people, the targets of my attack are truly the worst kind, the real scum of the earth, if I am careless and leave some sort of way to connect it back to me the consequences will be life or death.

A mistake could result in me turning up in pieces somewhere or taken and added into their prostitution ring forced to do ungodly things that make a shiver run down my spine, just thinking about it. If I don't do something though, I am just squandering my gifts, wasting my abilities. Today is the day I use them for something greater than myself. I know

I have taken precautions and it won't come back on me, but I understand my fear. I need to use that fear to fuel me, not to hinder me.

The school bell sounds. It's about a 30-minute casual walk home but I have a feeling that today won't take that long. My heart is pumping, the adrenaline has already kicked in for what is about to happen, my pace is definitely going to be faster than normal. I shove my books into my backpack and head directly for the door. I map out my path through the hallway and down the stairs before heading out the front foyer area, down the front path leading out the front gate of the school. I nearly made it all the way too, until a senior boy puts his arm out in front of me, stopping me just inside the gate.

'You're Sam, aren't you?' I nod. 'I'm told you can get things for people?' I look around to see who is around and don't see anything out of the norm. I look back at him and nod again. He reaches into his pocket and pulls out a handwritten note. It reads: *Fortnite super health and weapon upgrade will give you $30.* I consider for a moment, I am not a gamer but I know this is the current 'It' game that everyone's playing. Personally, I don't see the point. 100 people dropped on an island to kill each other off until the last one standing wins. It's pretty popular though, at least it's what most of the boys talk about and even some of the girls. I think the reason I am not interested in it is that it wouldn't be much of a challenge.

I look up at him and say, 'I'll need your log in and the fee is $50. In advance.' He looks at me as though he's considering arguing but something in the look on my face must have deter him. He takes a $50 note out of his wallet. He scribbles down his gamer login name on the bottom of the piece of paper he had previously handed me and then folds the money and paper together before passing it back to me. I stuff the note and money into my pocket and walk out the gate.

As I walk down the front of the school, I see a blacked-out SUV sitting across the road. It's a little out of place, but probably just some soccer mom's new wheels. I made great time home that day. It felt like it was only about 20 minutes. As I walk up the front stairs, the hairs on the back of my neck seem to stand on end. I retrieve my key from my pocket; it definitely feels like I am being watched but I can't see anything unusual. I think my project today is making me a bit paranoid. I shrug off the uneasy feeling and open the front door an shut it behind me locking the deadlock as it closed.

I make my way upstairs and drop my bag in the corner before making my way back downstairs to find a snack. I go for Coke and a couple of bags of snakes. Kind of my go-to for nights like this when I want to have a bit of a sugar buzz to ensure I am on my game. I might give myself an easy task first up and upgrade the jock's Fortnite account. I go over to my desk and open the lid on my laptop but before powering it on I lean over to the back right corner of my desk, with a bit of a push one of the boards slides out revealing a small opening. I reach in and pull out a small black bag. I look through the contents before finding my desired flash drive. I take it out and return the bag to the opening in the desk before sliding the board back into place.

I plug the USB drive into the laptop and power it on booting the unit from the Debian instance on the drive that has been customised for tasks such as this. As it fires up, my logon scripts start to run, most of them have been written in python to automate the anonymisation of my system. They essentially generate a random mac address, route my traffic through multiple VPN and anonymisation services. It's almost as though I was never here at all. I have got the configuration working so well. I fire up one of my tools and execute the shell connection I have for Fortnite, this isn't the first time I've been asked to do a bit of a power upgrade to a player's account. After a few minutes, I've turned the account into an almost unstoppable force. There won't be anyone who will be able to stop him unless they all gang up on him at once. Seems a bit pointless to me to want this. What is the point of the game if you can't die? You can barely get hurt. There would be zero challenge to the game anymore, you would achieve nothing other than a false sense of skill. People would think you are amazing at the game, a true elite but in reality, you are just cheating. But who am I to judge?

Now that the school homework is done it's time to get down to my real work, my job, my side hustle of sorts. I power off the machine, disconnect the USB drive and put it back in the black bag in the desk before retrieving tonight's drive. I created a custom machine for this purpose which is for nothing other than this job. Once the task has been completed, I will dissolve, erase the drive and rewrite it several times before hitting it with a hammer and then soaking the broken up pieces in saltwater. I will normally then take the pieces and drop them along a walk in the city, the pieces are so small that no one sees them but it scatters them around so well that even if someone knew what I was doing, they would never be able to piece it all back together. You never can be too cautious. Especially with the type of people I am about to piss off big time.

I power up the laptop, boot from the new drive and check over the configuration. I don't really need to check it as I have done so on at least three occasions before today to ensure it was ready. I load up my terminal and initiate command and control of my agents. I execute the attack sequence script and pause, looking at the blinking cursor on the screen, then after a moment a prompt pops up asking if I wish to execute the sequence.

I hesitate. There is no going back from this.

I hit enter and watch the sequence execute. The machines have been trickling all their data to a cloud platform for weeks and it was time to share the access with the Australian Federal Police or AFP for short and then destroy everything. Make the house burn down, so to speak.

I can only imagine what the people on the other end are going to be thinking. They would be in panic mode right now. Their systems would be locked and my modified version of ransomware virus will be locking everything down and erasing the data. The Kicker though is the sequence is then designed to max out all abilities of the systems and burn out the components. This will not only bring down the systems but will cost them greatly with all the hosted data centre equipment burning themselves out. I wonder if they will be smart enough to pull the plug before they let everything disintegrate.

Data flow to the cloud services has stopped and I see agents going offline. It's nearing the end of the road. I wonder if I will see any chatter about this over the coming days. Will it even be talked about? I think it will probably be swept away like it never happened. Crime syndicates like this wouldn't want to lose face about allowing something like this to happen. I know you are probably thinking that it won't make a difference, but if I can slow them down and save one girl from being taken advantage of by these scumbags or even slow down the distribution of the poor-quality drugs they keep selling then I have saved lives today. That's how I am justifying it to myself, anyway.

I stumbled across the group about six months earlier, they were selling girls for prostitution on one of dark web marketplaces. It's one of those places where money can literally buy you anything and has been where I have been choosing my targets from. Just trying to make a small difference in the world with the gifts I have. I can do things that law enforcement can't. I don't have any rules but my own moral compass. Why shouldn't I do something about these atrocities? I know it's illegal, I know I am putting myself in danger and I could spend a lot of time in jail if I was ever caught. But I think it's worth the risk.

A message pops up 'sequence complete'. No point stressing about it now, the jobs done. Cleanup time. I execute the sanitisation sequence on the drive and the laptop reboots into a new platform. After about 20 minutes, the drive is completely erased. I unplug the USB drive and boot the machine into windows. I open up my homework and then head downstairs to the garage.

It's smashing time.

Once the drive has been adequately pulverised, I collect the pieces in a small sunglasses bag I will keep in until I can take a walk to get rid of the evidence.

SUSPICION

IT'S 7 AM AND THE DREADED alarm goes off. I wack it a little harder than I probably should. I may have stayed up a little late with my celebrations for last night's project. I sat up till around 1 am watching a couple of old faithful movies, *Hackers* and then *Varsity Blues.* I really should have called it a night after *Hackers* finished but I was a little spooked after I heard some noises downstairs. I had a look around but couldn't see anything out of place. I think I was just a little paranoid after I took down the syndicate, I'm careful but you just never know. Anyway, no point getting caught up on what I should and shouldn't have done. It's time to crawl out of bed. I need to make myself presentable for the world and grab some breakfast.

I got ready for school quickly and tossed my bag over my shoulder. As I approach the front door to head off to school,

I freeze. The deadlock is open. I could have sworn I locked that when I came in last night. I stare at it for a few seconds. I mustn't have. I go through the front door and pull it closed behind me.

The morning goes by pretty quickly with not much of note happening until I'm sitting in English just before lunch and I look out the window. That same SUV I saw yesterday, is parked out just on the other side of our football oval. I can see it clearly from the second-floor window of the classroom. I see a slight glimmer of light coming from the passenger window, like the sun caught a phone screen or camera lens or something. Something just isn't right, I don't know exactly what it is but I will need to keep an eye out for that SUV in the future. If I can get the number plate, I will be able to see who it belongs to. Hacking the transport authority will be child's play, but it will set my suspicion at ease.

It's probably nothing, I am sure it will end up being a student's new ride or one of the staff at my school. I think taking down the syndicates systems has really made me paranoid. I need to get a grip, stop freaking myself out with everything.

Suddenly I hear my name, 'Samantha, what are your thoughts on the required reading?' I'm taken aback by the question.

'Sorry miss, I wasn't following.'

The teacher responds, 'I know Samantha, that's why I asked you. Please pay attention to what we are discussing. Have you at least read the book?'

I shake my head, 'Not all of it yet, miss.'

She looks annoyed but just shakes her head and continues with what she was doing before she chastised me. After a couple of minutes, I glanced back out the window and saw the SUV was gone. Maybe I am just being paranoid. Either way, I will just keep an eye out for it and see if I can get the plates. I try to pay better attention for the rest of the class, but I still find myself gazing out the window now and then. The topic just doesn't entertain me.

The bell sounds and I pack my stuff up to go to lunch. I go to the canteen and buy some lunch, then head over to sit with the other girls. Kate is one of my only real friends. She looks up at me and smiles when I sit next to her. We just go about eating our lunch with minimal chit chat, which is our thing, we aren't ones for a lot of talking. It's probably why we get along as well as we do. We don't mind a bit of silence. The awkward pause in the conversation that drives many crazy is our happy place.

Kate is my best friend, one of the few people I really trust. We just get each other and have been friends for as long as I can remember. I think I would be lost without her, my dad knows nothing about girls and without my mum around its good to have that person I can go to with things that I know would make my dad's skin crawl. He is good and he tries to be there for anything I need but he is still a guy and he has his limits. I respect that, so do I when it comes to what I feel comfortable with sharing with him. He is my dad afterall and things can get real awkward real fast.

I have never really told Kate what her friendship means to me. I am not one who likes to share how I feel, but I should really make the effort though before life at school comes to an end for us.

Out of nowhere, the guy from yesterday walks up to us with a sheepish grin on his face. I look over at Kate and she looks at me then looks at Michael, well I think that's his name anyway.

'Thanks for yesterday Sam, it helped.' He still has that awkward grin on his face. I look him in the eyes.

'That's great, can I help you with something else?' Kate knows a little about my night activities so I don't need to hide it.

He shuffles his feet for a couple of seconds and then awkwardly stumbles over his words, 'Well, umm, I was hoping you might want to go to a movie with me over the weekend?'

At that point, his face kind of turns a warm red colour. I look over to his right side and I can see some of his friends laughing and whispering something behind him. They must know what he was coming over to ask. The silence stretches for almost a minute before he stumbles over the same sentence again. I look over at Kate and see that she is doing everything she can not to burst out in laughter, so she isn't going to be any help to me.

He is getting more and more fidgety, if I don't give him a response soon, I think he might die of shame. Strangely, for the first time in forever, I'm not entirely repulsed by the idea. What the heck, it's only a movie, right? I look up at him.

'It's Michael. Isn't it?' he nods and I continue, 'Okay but I get to pick the movie.' A grin from ear to ear starts to form on his face and I hope I haven't made a mistake. He reaches into his pocket, pulls out his phone and unlocks it then hands it to me.

'Can I have your number so I can text you about it?' I take the phone and put in my number and hand it back to him. He stands there for a few seconds looking at me and then realises that it's getting a bit weird before blurting, 'Okay great, I will text you later. I better go.' I just half-smile and nod. I am so going to regret this.

As soon as he walks away, Kate bursts into laughter, she is enjoying this, probably a little too much. Once she recovers all she can manage to say is, 'He's hot. If you don't want him I'll have him.' I just raise my eyebrows at her while she keeps rolling around with laughter. Literally. The rest of the day passes by pretty uneventful with Kate giving me a hard time about Michael asking me out. Honestly though, I don't even know why I said yes, I think I felt sorry for him a little with how awkward he looked. It's only one date and then I can just go back to ignoring him.

The school day finally comes to an end. I started to walk home again as normal, responding to a couple of texts from Michael about going to the movies on Friday night. I'm going to have to tell my father I am going on a date. That's going to be a fun conversation. I take a deep breath and try to calm myself. It's surely not going to be that bad.

I hope.

As I go around the corner in my street, I see a glimpse of a black car parked up the street from my house. I take care not to look at it directly. I take a subtle look at the number plate, well at least I think it is subtle and make a mental note of the details. I am going to check who owns it when I get upstairs. Maybe my criminal friends from last night are onto me.

In my room, I get out one of my Debian machine drives from within my desk. I get straight to work finding my target at the transport authority. I look through the company employees on Facebook and LinkedIn. Suddenly I have a target. Felicity, in administration. I send out an email to one of her accounts with a quickly put together sales promotion for a bookstore, one that she talks about a lot on her socials and offer a 30% deal on the book she was just this morning saying she wanted to read. She will think it's her lucky day until the promo code doesn't work on the site.

I feel like I should feel bad for invading her privacy, for digging into her life, using her as my means to an end. Strangely I don't though, in the cyber world there is a sort of disconnect. Yes, I know Felicity is a person and from what I can see a reasonably good person. I know if my breach of the transport authority is detected she could get in trouble for it and there could be some consequences for her. But I need to know who it is following me though, this could literally be life of death.

She gets the email and clicks on the link. As soon as she does that, it loads my command and control system before then redirecting her back to the real book store which doesn't have a sale on the book. I wait for her to look around for a few minutes before I execute the webcam and mic on the machine, so I know when it is safe to check out the machine. It's probably thirty minutes before she leaves the room and another thirty before I decide it's safe to poke around. She still ended up buying the book, even without my fake discount.

Bingo; she has remote access configured for work with saved credentials. I pull the saved config onto my virtual machine, clone her IP and mac address so that when I connect to the remote location, it will look like Felicity. I connect and open up the vehicle registration system, I hope I am not making a mistake by doing this, I haven't planned this, it's very adhoc. I probably shouldn't have broken into the transport system but it's too late now. If I make a mistake and leave something that could connect me to this could get me into a world of trouble. All over some paranoia but I guess I am already in. I might as well finish what I started.

I punch the rego plate into the systems, PKR-601 and wait for the response. After a few seconds, it responds with an unlisted plate, government-owned. I think at that point I turn a slight shade whiter. Am I finally being busted? Have I made a mistake? Do they know everything I have done? What am I going to say to Dad? Oh, this is not good. I hadn't even considered the AFP coming after me, I was just paranoid about the crime syndicate.

I take a deep breath again and make my way over to the window to see if the car is still parked down the street. The SUV is gone. I don't know if I should be relieved or not that it's gone. Am I just being paranoid about all of this? I back out of the systems and clean my tracks as I go, then power down the laptop and put the flash drive back in the secret spot in the table. I wonder if they were at our house last night, I thought I was just being jumpy because of what I had just done but maybe I wasn't hearing things. Maybe someone was really in my house last night.

Oh crap, what if they have bugged our house.

I take out a frequency scanner from my drawer, I know it's weird that I have one. I do though, with the things I get up to in my spare time you can never be to paranoid. I got it a few years ago after I started going after targets like last night, none of them have been that sort of scale but I wanted to make sure that I was taking all of the right precautions. Since I have it, I should do a full sweep of the house. I checked every room and nothing. Maybe I am just paranoid and they weren't even following me. Maybe they are just a government employee with a company car who just visited someone they know down the street. That's probably more likely than some government cyber squad on the hunt for me. I have always been careful. They wouldn't even know I exist.

I need to get rid of the evidence from last night though, just to be sure. I've got it. Date night. Brilliant. I take out my phone and text Michael that I would like to catch a movie tonight, instead of Friday.

He takes seconds to respond, 'I would love to. Text me your address and I will pick you up.' That was a fast, I hope I am not making this whole situation worse, making him feel this is more than it is. Is it more, if I really think about it, is that why I opted for the date night idea? Do I like him more than I want to admit, I start to get a bit of a flutter in my stomach, maybe it is more than just making the awkward situation go away? It's not the first time someone had asked me out, it was the only time I had ever agreed though.

I text him my address and after about 20 minutes he arrives at my house in what looks to be his parent's car. He must have borrowed it for the date. I meet him out the front; I glance down the street but don't see the SUV. He jumps out of the car and runs around to open the passenger's car door and I smile at him. I suddenly feel very nervous as I get in and reach for my seatbelt. The door move was kind of sweet, something her dad would probably do on a date. He must be as nervous as I am right now. Don't get to distracted Sam, this date is about getting rid of the drive and any evidence that could link me to anything that happened yesterday.

When we get out at the cinemas, I retrieve the glasses bag from my pocket and slowly start to drop pieces as we walk down the street. By the time we reach the front of the cinema the bag is empty and we enter the building. The date went quite well and I even let Michael hold my hand during the movie. I surprised myself a little with that. I am not even sure what movie we saw; we talked softly through most of it. Some of the other moviegoers were not impressed about that though we got shushed a few times. I was a little worried he was going to try and kiss me when he dropped me home after the movie. It looked like he was considering it but he must of chickened out, I am actually glad he did. I am not really sure I was ready for that.

A few days go by without seeing the SUV again. I've been texting Michael a little and had to admit to Dad that I had gone on a date. He looked quite pale when I told him. I don't think he is ready for me to date yet. He insisted he meet him but I said maybe once I know if it's a thing or not. He begrudgingly agreed and things continued on this way for a couple of weeks, until I got called to the principal's office one day during class. I'm not sure where this is going, but I have a bad feeling.

THE PRINCIPAL'S OFFICE

IT'S THE FIRST TIME I have been to the front office of the school for anything other than paying for my school fees or excursions but dad does most of that online these days. I even had to ask at the front desk where the principal's office was. The chairs outside of the office look old and worn. I guess I must be one of the rare students who doesn't have regular visits.

I have been sitting here for about 20 minutes. I can hear someone inside being chastised about their poor judgement and how it will probably ruin their chances of getting into a good university. I guess whatever it is that I am here for, it isn't going to be pleasant. I fiddle around in my bag to see if I have anything to snack on while I wait, but I don't find anything that interests me, just a blackening banana that has probably been in my bag a little too long. I see a bin in the corner and I toss the banana in. It makes a weird thud noise a little louder than I anticipated. The girl sitting across from me reading a magazine gives me a strange look before continuing to read.

Suddenly the door opens and a boy from my year exits a little too quickly and almost runs straight into me. His eyes are puffy and his nose looks slightly damp, I think he's been crying. The deputy must be a real ball breaker. This should be fun. The boy pauses for a few seconds, wipes his nose on his sleeve, straightens and turns toward the hallway leading out of the waiting room.

'Samantha, come in please' a voice demands from within the office, little louder than I was expecting and I jumped a little. Pull yourself together, don't give anything away.

I stand and walk through the door and I see a lady probably in her early forties maybe, which is younger than I expected. She is a little stuffy looking, but quite pretty, really. She gestures for me to sit in one of the two chairs in front of her desk, so I do as directed. I look around the room as I sit down and it is a very minimalistic look with very few personal items or personalisation of the room at all. It's almost clinical. I look up after a few seconds and realise that she has been watching me the whole time and it makes me feel a little awkward, if I am honest. I just want to know what this is all about so I can take my punishment and get out of here.

She keeps looking at me, holding my gaze for another 10 seconds, possibly seeing if I would drop my eyes first, but that isn't something I would do even if I'm a little uncomfortable.

'Do you know why you are here Samantha?' she finally says.

'It's just Sam. No one calls me Samantha except my father.' She looks at me and I can almost see her deciding what path to take with me and then it looks as though she decides to take an easy tone. She turns her chair slightly and looks out the single window in her office.

She looks as though she is pondering something for a moment, just staring out that window when she turns suddenly back towards me, reaches for something under a pile of books.

'I think you should take a look at this,' and then turns back towards the window before continuing, 'I was made aware of this competition coming up next week in Brisbane that I feel you should consider competing in.' I glance down at the piece of paper and I can see that it is a government - Hack the World event. I have seen them being discussed on the news a few months ago, but I thought they were a bit stupid. Why would I want to go to one of these competitions and put a target on my back by the feds? Doesn't make sense.

I look up and try to put a confused look on my face, 'I don't understand, sorry. Why would I want to compete in this competition?'

After a few moments she says, 'We both know you have the skills.' I was a little thrown by the statement, what does she know? I need to be careful how I respond, I don't want to give anything away. She looks at me and grins. Now I really want to know what she knows. It can't be good.

'I have worked here for many years and I have never had you in my office. From what I can see in your school record, you are the clear definition of average. I think it's all a lie.' She pauses again for a few moments and just as I am preparing to answer she continues, 'Today I was told that you have quite a gift. You are the person that can get things for people. Whatever they need, you can get it. You apparently have a true skill with these computer things, yet you haven't taken a single computer class. Can you tell me why that is?'

I wasn't sure how I should answer this but I figured short and honest would be best 'I haven't taken any computer classes because I wouldn't have learnt anything' and then continued to read over the flyer. We both sit in silence for a few minutes considering our positions. Well, that's what I was doing anyway before I said, 'have I done something wrong?' She stares at me, not in a hostile way but more like I'm a curiosity.

'I have two choices with you, Sam. I could punish you and report you to law enforcement for the illegal things that we both know you have been doing for students, or I could take the advice I was given and let you represent our school in this competition next week. What do you think I should do?'

I'm not sure exactly how I got into this situation but now I'm here, I need to figure out the best option.

After a few moments, I decide, 'I think the competition sounds like the best option but my father will never agree to me going. I don't think it's something we can afford.' She smiles at me again in a way that almost says I have got you now.

'I have already discussed the competition with your father and he has agreed to you representing the school. He also said that he was quite surprised at your apparent abilities. He was never aware that you were so gifted.' Oh crap, they have already talked to Dad. I am so dead.

She continues, 'As for the costs, everything will be covered by the school. It won't cost you or your father anything. However, you could win ten thousand dollars for the school and your choice of new computer equipment for yourself, also to the value of ten thousand dollars.' Now, that sounds pretty sweet. I could do with a power upgrade and this way I could buy the best and Dad wouldn't get suspicious. Sounds like a win, win situation really. I get out of this bind I am in, get the school some cash and get a new beefed-up computer. I just have to be careful not to give too much away during the competition or people will find out too much about my extracurricular activities.

'So what have you decided, Sam? Do you want to take the red pill or the blue pill?' I almost burst out with laughter with that comment. A teacher who actually has a matrix reference. Classic. She shrugs slightly amused herself, 'I suspected you'd get the reference. Red pill, I suspend you and tell your father you are doing illegal favours for students. Or the blue pill and you go down the rabbit hole, to the competition.' I couldn't help but giggle a little and I didn't need to think, it was a no brainer.

'I only see one choice really; I will take the blue pill.'

She smiles at me again and stands up, 'I knew you would make the right choice, Sam. I will have everything organised and have the travel details sent to your house so your father can see everything as well.' I nod and she reaches out with her hand and I take it. It was a firm shake. She is a smart woman, that I could tell already and she is used to getting what she wants. She releases my hand and then gestures to the door. 'I look forward to hearing about the cash injection from your win Sam. Do us proud.'

I leave her office, still a bit confused as to how that all came about and how exactly I ended up getting signed up for this weird capture the flag/hacking event in Brisbane. Tonight, I am certain I will have twenty questions from my dad about my mysterious hidden skill. I will need to be careful about what I say, otherwise I might lose some of that freedom I am used to.

THE COMPETITION

I AM JUST LAYING on my bed looking up at the roof letting my mind run crazy with possible scenarios, what obstacles would there be for me to overcome? Would there finally be a system I can't break into? The idea I would not be able to defeat it excites me. I want a challenge I can't overcome, something to make me dig deep and put in everything I have to overthrow the obstacle. Who knows what it will be, but I need to remember that yes, I can have fun with this, but I can't reveal myself to anyone. I need to stay safe, Dad's safety depends on it as much as mine does.

I look over at the alarm clock and it flicks over to 6 am. I am never awake this early. I must be excited about the challenge today. I hear a noise downstairs as Dad starts to make some breakfast. He told me last night he was going to make me a full English breakfast so I had all the brain food

I needed for the competition. He has been pretty excited by the whole idea that I am some kind of computer genius. I don't think I am anything special but I just let him enjoy the moment. I think he deserves that, for what he does for me. If I win the competition, there will be no changing his mind.

I get dressed, pack my laptop and make my way downstairs to have breakfast. I deliberately left most of my best tools and Linux distros in the compartment in my desk. I don't want to use any of the same tools or scripts I have used in my previous hacker activities. I will do it blind today and have no connection to any of that part of my other life. That should make it a bit harder, so I don't draw too much attention to myself.

Foresight needs to stay a secret. I walk into the kitchen and my dad looks at me and gestures towards the table.

'Sit down it is almost ready.' I do as he asks. I place my laptop on the end of the kitchen bench. As I do he looks over at it, 'so that's where all the magic happens hey?'

I smile, 'Something like that Dad'.

We eat our breakfast in relative silence with some idle chit chat now and then, but nothing of note. We pack up the kitchen, switch on the dishwasher and then we pile in Dad's truck to make our way down to Brisbane city. The competition starts at 9 am but Dad said we should get a head start as traffic is always bad heading into the city. He was right. I think a snail could have moved faster than we could down the highway in some places. When we finally get there, Dad drives me up to the front entrance before telling me he will find a park and for me to go get myself all sorted inside. He would find a spot to watch so he doesn't cramp my style. I roll my eyes a little at that last point but don't comment. I will never be embarrassed by Dad.

I get out of the truck and walk through the front doors of the convention centre, wow there are people everywhere. I am a little surprised. This is a big deal. I was expecting about 100 geeks and some family members to support them. All dungeons and dragons playing geeks, you know who I'm talking about. I should know better than to stereotype people though, I am one of those walking contradictions. I am nothing like what most people would think of when someone says, hacker. I look around and yes, I see a couple of true geeks, but most are just normal looking people.

I weave my way through the crowd and after a few minutes I see the registration desk. After a few minutes wait, I am next to the desk.

'Can I help you, Miss?' I reach down and pull out the paperwork I was given from the school with my registration and hand it over. She looks at the documentation and then looks back up at me. 'Do you have any ID?' that's a bit strange but I reach in and pull out my driver's licence, I got it a few months ago but don't use it. It's not because I don't want to drive or anything, Dad's truck is the only car we have and I can't just go out and buy one. I think that would raise some eyebrows and I am not sure my dad would understand how I would be able to afford one. I love cars and I will get myself something fun after I head off to university or get a job. My dad said the licence would come in handy when I get a job or go to university and it turns out it is already being useful.

She looks it over and then hands it back before going about her business for a few more minutes. I look around why I wait for her to finish and don't see any familiar faces. However, at the far back of the room, I see a couple of government looking people talking to someone that looks like he is military. As I look over at him, he catches my eye.

He holds it and doesn't avert his gaze. He is a confident proud soldier who oozes authority. He looks like he is in his mid-50s and has had a hard life. You can just see it in his face. It starts to feel a little weird, so I turn and look back at the lady working away at the registration desk.

She gathers up a few things and starts to make her way back over to me.

'Samantha, please make your way down to that room on the left where the main competition will start at 10 am.' She points to the room past where the soldier was standing. He's gone now. 'You will have five hours to complete as much of the competition as you can. The rules and instructions will be provided to all participants before the start of events.' I nod and take the identification badge and put the lanyard over my head. I collect together the rest of the paperwork and make my way towards the room.

I walk up to the security guys at the door and show them my ID and they let me through to an usher who directs me to my designated desk that is labelled with the school's name. I look around and there are around 30 more desks with 3-4 seats at each one with other schools marked on them. At my desk only one seat is placed so I won't be getting any teammates which I am pleased about. I prefer to work alone, with fewer eyes looking over what I am doing.

I pull out my laptop and start getting everything set up, as I am plugging it into the network, I see the military guy from the main area come through the same door I just entered through. He is surrounded by several bodyguards, from what I can tell. He sees me and leans over and whispers something to one of them. They turn and look at me before turning back and nodding to him. He turns and walks towards the main stage at the front of the room. The bodyguards follow suit except for the one who looked over at me. He turns and heads towards me. I am not sure what he wants, but he freaks me out a little.

When he arrives at my desk, he pauses in front of me, he waits till I lift my gaze to look at him.

'Excuse me, Samantha, I have been instructed to wish you well for today's competition. The general has indicated that he looks forward to seeing what you can do and that he has heard interesting things about you. He would like to see if it's all true or not.'

I am a little surprised at that statement. A general knows about me and what I can do. I don't know if it's a good thing or not. Too late to back out now, Dad will be very disappointed if I drop out of the competition. I only have one option.

'Thanks, I will do my best to impress the general,' I say, with a bit of a goofy smile. The human shield nods at me.

'I will let him know.' He walks back towards the general, his steps brisk. Wow, he took that very literally. He did not pick up any of the sarcasm that I was laying on thick. I should be more careful about what I say to people. I shrug it off and continue with what I was doing before the interruption.

A few minutes later the room fills with a flood of competitors and their supporters. I see Dad come in and head towards the back of the room. He looks a bit like a deer in headlights, not sure where to look or go. He sees me watching him and he smiles, and straightens his shoulders, I guess to make me feel a bit better about the whole situation. Surprisingly even though I know it was fake and that he did it for my sake, it does make me relax a little.

Tap Tap Tap, 'Is this on?' Someone is on the main stage and they start to discuss the proceedings of the day. Some general rules of what is acceptable and how long we have to achieve the target milestones. They also talked about a secret level for anyone who finished the competition early, a way to double the prize pack. I have an uncontrollable urge to beat that target, crush my opponents and walk out with the double prize pool. They go on to comment about being grateful for the support of General James O'Connor from the Australian Defence force cyber command for this event. I still think it's strange that General James has taken an interest in me. What could he possibly want from a 17-year-old hacker?

After about ten minutes of fluff, they start the clock. 'Your five hours starts now.' I am looking forward to this. It's time to dig deep and smash my way through these systems. It's refreshing not to need to be stealthy and clean my tracks, I just need to reach my target. Double prize bounty, here we come.

CRUSHING MY OPPONENTS

THE ANNOUNCEMENT STARTS a frenzy of activity. Most in the competition are in teams of three or more and are all banging away on their keyboards. They're reminding me of the people in movies in all those hacking scenes. You know the ones where the hacker just smashes the keys randomly. Looking around at my competitors, I guess there's a reason why the stereotype exists.

I see people using windows and some on Linux distros like Kali or some other popular pentest distribution. I have even seen a couple of tablets with Nethunter. I don't know why they think that will be useful, but each to their own. I realise that I have been sitting here looking around, seeing what others are doing for about 15 minutes, maybe I should focus a little and get to work.

I take a deep breath and look over at Dad, he meets

my gaze and gives me a thumbs up. I think he mouths to me, 'You got this.' He has faith in me. I take another deep breath and boot up my machine, let's get this show on the road.

I open a terminal on my machine and kick off a network crawl. I want to know what I am getting into here. I see a list of systems like SQL databases, webservers, PCs and some miscellaneous servers. I can see the versions of software with obvious vulnerabilities. Maybe this isn't going to be much of a challenge after all. I work my way through the systems, knocking them over one by one until they are all done except for one pc. I smash my way through its protections and just look at the screen. That was too easy.

I look up and glance around the room. Everyone else is still in their little huddles, trying to work their way through the obstacles set out for them. As I continue to look around, I see the clock at the front of the room and it still has 3 hours and 38 minutes left. That only took me a little over an hour.

It can't be this easy. There must have been something I missed. I take a closer look at the final desktop. Why would they make this machine the final obstacle in the challenge? It was simple. It hadn't been patched ever and was just a basic Windows 10 system. What am I missing...?

I check through the network configuration and see that it has a dual IP. Maybe it is a gateway to another isolated network. I load some tools and do a scan of the network range. There are some servers just sitting there. I check them out cautiously. Something about this isn't right. I load up Wireshark and monitor the traffic in and out of the server's bingo. They are honey pots ready to distract me from the real surprise 192.168.10.189, the IP address of where all the data is being sent back through too. I check it out and there is a firewall between me and the end device. I do some light touch work on the firewall and it turns out that it is cisco, one that hasn't been patched.

That's my in. I check to see if it is vulnerable to any known attacks. I attempt to access the web portal and I see it is vulnerable to credential caching. If I can execute an export command, it will allow me to pull the last admin login details used. I put together a rough script to do what I need and pause. I don't think this is the extra part of the game. I think that this is the backend systems that are being used to monitor the game. Do I stop or do I go for it? I can crush my opponents and the people who are running the competition.

I consider for a moment, taking things to the next level could show my hand but I want to do my best, I want to show dad that he can be proud of me. I can see him watching me. Oh screw it, I want that double prize pool. I want to make him proud.

I execute the script and pull the admin credentials. I log onto the firewall and reveal the VPN credentials. I use them to gain an active connection to the network and do a soft crawl and this is defence gear. Oh crap, I don't know if this was a good idea after all, but this is the name of the game, isn't it? Crush all obstacles in my path. Capture all flags and systems on my way. So I make my way through the network and find my way in with a weak set of credentials. I log on with the user account and decide to have a little fun.

I load a screensaver on the main pc that is displaying the event details up on the main stage. It's there to display updates for the event. I load a video that will have a skater chick who lands an awesome trick and then rushes the screen shouting you have been owned. After a few seconds of pause, I decided to add a tag line with my school's name on it at the end and execute. If I am going to go big, I might as well go all in. I pull back from the systems and just relax in my chair with a goofy grin on my face.

I look around and see the general looking over in my direction and he is talking to one of his team. He nods at me with a sort of acknowledgement. They know what I have gotten access to. Maybe they are trying to figure out what I did. Suddenly the video plays on the big screen and a smile creeps onto the general's face. I look over at the clock. 2 hours 58 minutes remaining. I see him signal for one of his team and suddenly the video disappears. My school suddenly jumps to the top of the leader board with a time of 2 hours 2 minutes listed next to it. With a bonus round star tagged and a blinking winner icon.

A few moments later, someone comes on stage and informs everyone that the winner of the competition has been decided and places two and three are still up for grabs. Keep working hard on the objectives. I look over at Dad and he has a blend of astonishment and pride written all over his face. I think there will be no changing his mind that I am some sort of computer genius now. I smile at him and he nods at me mouthing, 'nice work, I am so proud of you.' I feel a flush of pride at that moment and I forget about the unwanted attention that I have probably just brought on myself.

I glance toward the general again and I see him whispering something to the human shield that talked to me initially. He starts to make his way towards me. Here we go. When he arrives in front of my desk he pauses again waiting for me to look up at him.

'Samantha, the general would like to have a word with you in private for a moment. Please follow me.' The look on his face didn't seem to me as though the request was optional. I rise and follow him to a door at the side of the main room. He opens the door and as I walk through the general is standing to one side talking to the guy that he asked to pull my video from the main screen.

He meets my gaze as the door is pulled closed behind me with a thud.

'Miss Erkhart. Quite a show you put on today.' I nod. 'I had heard you were good, but 2 hours 2 minutes and you breached the private network that wasn't even supposed to be part of the game.' He walks over to me until he's less than a few feet away. 'What gave the honey pot away? Why did you change your target? We could see you checking it out then just like that, you changed direction.'

I consider my answer. Everyone in the room was waiting to see what I would say. 'Your concealment of the logging traffic was bad. You should have only been transmitting major alerts back to control and stored the rest on the device for later review. Too much traffic was unusual. It just felt off.' I grimaced at the general. 'I think your team could have made the objectives a bit harder, don't you think?' I heard a slight chuckle from someone behind me at that point, who received a sharp glare from the general. It stopped instantly.

'Miss Erkhart, let me tell you something, the 29 other teams out there haven't even passed stage 4, and you have taken out the entire 10 stages, pushed into the bonus network as well as broke through to the secure network. I think the only person who found it easy was you.' He reaches for something inside his coat jacket and pulls out a card, handing it to me. All it has is a phone number. 'If you would like to discuss an opportunity for after you graduate in a few weeks, give this number a call, tell them the general sent you.' He looks at his man behind me and nods. The human shield opens the door behind me and tells me it's time to head back to the competition.

As I walk through the door, I see Dad arguing with one of the bodyguards, asking why they are talking to me in the room without his presence. He looks up and sees me. I smile and wave at him.

'Are you okay honey, what was going on in there?' He asks as he reaches my side. I shrug.

'They were just interested in my techniques and how I defeated their defences so fast. I just told them it was because they didn't really have any defences, maybe they should do better next time.' Dad's shoulders seem to relax a little. 'Do you want to wait with me at my desk until everyone else finishes?' he nods.

'Of course I would. It will put me closer to the action and will make it easier to take some pictures of you getting your prize.'

It has been an interesting day. My head is spinning with what has occurred and the card the general gave me was almost burning my skin. I want to call and find out what's on offer but I probably shouldn't. It's too much of a risk. Isn't it?

TAKING HOME THE LOOT

I PACK UP MY COMPUTER equipment while I wait for the competition to end, if I didn't have to wait for the prizes I would bail but I don't have much choice. If I want the $10k in cash and $10k voucher for new computer equipment, I need to stay until they hand out the prizes. I think the principal should be happy I have won the school $20K worth of school equipment. That should help to bring the computer lab into the 21st century. Maybe they might name the lab after me, that's an odd thought. I truly hope they don't do that.

I must be staring off into space, as when I look over to Dad, he asked if I was okay.

'Yes, I am fine Dad, I am just daydreaming, thinking about what kind of new computer system I can get with $10K.' He smiles. 'I am glad you came with me today, it made me feel at ease and want to do my best.'

Dad looks at me with the biggest smile on his face and gives me a sideways hug, one arm wrapped around my shoulders. 'It was my pleasure, Sam, I would never have missed this.' I grin, but shrug out of his embrace. As I put the last few items in my bag, I notice I am being watched. As I look around the room, quite a few of the other school teams are outright glaring at me. It's getting a little weird.

Another hour passes, the competition finally ends and the winners are announced officially. We are brought up on stage and given our prize packs while constant flashing of the camera's record every moment. I smile and go through the motions as required, but as soon as it is socially acceptable, I return to Dad. 'Let's get out of here!' I say and we gather everything up and head for the door. The main foyer area that was filled with people this morning is now more like a ghost town than a bustling event, I guess everyone got what they came for. Dad points towards the elevator and we head down to level four of the car park.

As I exit the elevator, I see something in the far corner of my vision. It's that black SUV that I have been seeing around the school and in our street. I don't want to look over in case I give myself away. Dad points towards the back corner of the car park and tells me the car is parked over there. I barely acknowledge his statement as I am too concerned about that SUV and what is it doing here? Am I still being watched?

I pick up my pace a little to get to the car as quickly as I can without making it too obvious. Dad notices though and looks over at me a little puzzled, 'are you in a hurry to get somewhere?' I look back at him and consider if I should tell him about the SUV or will that just freak him out? I will keep it to myself for now, but if it gets out of hand, I will bring him into the loop. 'There is a great computer store on the way home and I was hoping we might get there early enough to check out some upgrade options.'

He instantly smiles, 'of course. Anything for my super hacker genius daughter.' I force myself to smile and pick up the pace a little more, and thankfully, he does the same.

We reach the car and we both pile in. I grab my seat belt and fasten myself in. I look back over to the SUV as we make our way out of the underground car park. I can see movement. There are several figures in it but the tint is too dark to make anything particular out. I hope it's nothing to do with what I did the other day. If I have put Dad at risk, I will never forgive myself.

As we start our ascent out of the car park, the lights on the SUV switch on. Someone has just started the engine and I see in my side mirror that it has started to pull out of the park. As we continue to make our way out I see several flashes of light from the SUV behind us slowly making its way behind us. We finally reach the final exit gate and dad puts his window down to insert our parking card; he prepaid for the day's parking that morning. As he does his thing with the gate, I see the SUV pull up to the gate beside us. The window starts to move down. This is my chance to see who it is that seems to be following me. I can see the top of the driver's head appear; they have brown hair. Here we go. Suddenly, Dad surges forward and the view of the SUV is gone. No, no, no! That might have been my only chance to find out who it is that's tailing me.

Argh, I guess it wasn't meant to be. We pull out of the driveway and Dad makes his way back towards home. He turns to me after a few minutes, 'Let me know where you want to go hacker shopping?' I really won't live this one down now. Maybe the new computer wasn't worth it, after all. I think I preferred it when Dad had no idea about my skills. I will probably be stuck fixing all of his work friend's computers now, as he will more than likely brag about how great I am with computers.

I just nod, and we continue to drive in relative silence for almost 30 minutes before I give him some direction to the computer store. When we pull up in the car park, I glance around to check for the SUV. Please, please make it that I am just paranoid and it isn't following us. I take a deep breath and almost sigh with relief when it is nowhere to be seen. I am just delusional and maybe a bit paranoid. Maybe I just need to get some more sleep at nights instead of doing dangerous things as Foresight.

I walk around the store almost like a little kid in a candy shop. I can get so much with my prize money. I put a bit of a list together in my head before looking over to the guy at the counter.

'Can you help me place an order?'

He gives me a bit of a look over and says, 'what sort of thing do you want to do honey?' Honey? Oh that's not cool. He continues, 'Play music? Social media? Maybe watch some movies or YouTube or something?' Oh, this guy is going to cop it. I look over at Dad for a moment and he has this look of anticipation, like he is waiting for the bomb to explode. He knows me way too well.

I look back at the guy behind the counter and eye the name badge on his chest.

'Jack, is it?' he nods. 'Do me a favour, would you? Pull your head out of your arse for a moment and listen.' The look on his face changes. He doesn't think he is so smooth now. 'Just because I am a girl it doesn't mean that I don't know anything about computers, I just won the prize that this store's head office donated to a capture the flag contest in the city. If you call me HONEY one more time, I will make sure that everyone in the state knows what you get up to on your computer when you are alone.' I feel a little bad right now as he looks as though he is either going to cry or worse, wet himself. I look at him for a moment longer before continuing. 'Now, do you need to write my order down?' he nods and grabs a pad and paper.

'I want Asus Maximus XI hero motherboard, NVidia GeForce RTX 2080 Ti video card and I want the best RAM you can get me and as much as you can fit on the board'. I add a large SSD and about 10TB worth of additional storage and an Intel Core i9 processor to drive it all. I add a see-through gamer case that can hold all of my new gear and even splurge out on a 49' super ultra-wide curved screen. This thing is going to be a nice machine.

I turn to look at Dad and he has a glazed look on his face. I think I have lost him. I look back at Jack the jerk behind the counter and he looks almost impressed. He finishes writing my list out, 'we have all of this in stock do you want me to get it all ready for you now?' The look on my face must have answered his question, as he just nods and busies himself with gathering my order. I watch him zig-zag through the storage area behind the counter collecting my items and after about 10 minutes he returns with a trolley full of stuff.

'Miss, I have upgraded your power supply, cooling system and will add in an LED package for your case for no extra charge. What colour would you like?' I point to the blue kit and he adds it to my collection. 'Do you have your voucher number from your prize?' I reach into my pocket and collect the voucher and hand it over to him. 'Wow, that's an impressive prize. I assume we will be seeing you again,

Samantha, you are going to have quite a lot left to spend after this order' I don't think I will need anything else, maybe I could buy Dad a laptop and they sell big screen TV's that could be a good choice. I think the 32' we have now could do with an upgrade.

Jack puts it all through the register and then offers to help take it to the car, which we agree to. We load it all in and start our drive back home. It was a good day today, a really good day, especially for Dad and me. This whole event seems to have been a great bonding moment for us. It puts a bit of a smile on my face as I think about it.

MEETING JAMES

IT'S BEEN A FEW DAYS since the competition now and my father is still hyped up about the whole experience. I could do anything I wanted and he would still be happy with me. He even agreed to me going out with Michael tonight. He said that I had earned a bit of fun with all of my hard work at the competition. I don't have the heart to tell him that to me it was easy. I still don't know how my gift works, but it's like I just close my eyes and visualise and the machines do what I want. Like I can control them almost with my mind.

I know it sounds weird, but I have been hiding this gift of mine for years and now it's out in the open. Well it's mostly out in the open. People just think I am a super hacker or something, which is partly true. I am a very skilled hacker. But I am not your normal hacker. I am Foresight.

I hear a knock at the door. It must be Michael. He is taking me to see a movie, I don't even know what it is we are supposed to be watching, but it will be good to just chill out for a while. I check my hair and outfit in the mirror before turning for the door. I make my way downstairs and see Michael sitting at the kitchen table with Dad.

'Dad, I hope you aren't giving Michael a hard time or anything?' A small grin creeps onto his face. There's a churning feeling in my stomach and I can see from Michael's face that Dad's been stirring him up a little. 'I just told Michael that I have a shovel in the garage and if I hear that he so much as touches a single hair on your head, I will be burying him in my backyard with it. That's all Sam.' I fight back a giggle but can't hide the smile which Dad sees. It makes his smile stretch right across his face.

'Bye Dad. I will be back before midnight. Michael let's go before he tells you about his guns' Dad's smile gets bigger, if it's even possible. I shouldn't encourage him though. He stops though after a few seconds, 'Your curfew is 11 pm Sam, not 12. Make sure your home by 11 please' it was worth a try but I just nod. I look over at Michael and instantly he gets up and we walk out the front door. We look over at each other while we walk down the front path. He opens my door as we approach his car. It's a short drive to the cinema and when we arrived, Michael quickly jumps out to open my door for me again, he is pulling out the gentlemanly acts tonight. Michael might be a good guy; I might have found a really good one here but I shouldn't get ahead of myself. I am still not sure I am ready for a relationship, but I am going with it for now.

We start to walk to the cinemas and he reaches to take my hand. I let him. It's strange, I have this weird butterfly sensation in my stomach and it sort of tingles around the areas where our skin touches. I don't understand this whole teenage hormone stuff, this is all alien to me. I would be less scared to hack the DoD than I would be to kiss Michael tonight. I know it is a possibility he will try at some point and I think I am okay with it, but it terrifies me a little.

The movie goes by fast. It's some sort of teenage rom-com. I don't even remember the name. I was freaking out the whole time as a few minutes in Michael, moved from holding my hand and placed his hand on the inside of my thigh, high up on my leg. There was a warm tingly sensation right up the inner part of my leg and it almost burned where his hand rested. It was exhilarating and terrifying at the same time. I was almost frozen, was I ready for this? Did I want to get more physical with Michael? And would a kiss be enough? What was he expecting?

The movie finished and we walked in silence to the car, a sort of anticipation that something was going to happen in the air. When we get to his car, I see him look at the door and in anticipation that he will open the door for me again, I turn to the side and hesitate. As I do, I think Michael took it as me giving him a cue, a green light? He turns toward me and places his hands on my hips. He gently guides me and I feel myself bump into his car coming to rest on it, when I do, he slides his hands slowly up from my waist, sliding them under the bottom edge of my shirt. As his hands slide onto my bare skin, I can feel the tingling sensation spread across most of my body. I don't want him to stop there, I want him to touch me everywhere. These clothes between us are frustrating me, I want to feel his skin on mine and I want to feel this sensation spread across every nerve in my body. I want to lose control, just a little.

He presses his body against mine and leans forward. He is going to kiss me. I look at his lips as they near mine, They look gentle but determined. They meet with mine after what feels like minutes. They feel soft to touch, moist and inviting. I feel a strong desire to claw at his clothes as he pulls back and slightly parts his lips, then locks them with mine again. I feel a little short of breath. I didn't know this is what it would feel like. It feels like a drug is entering my system, like an addiction I know will be hard to kick.

Suddenly, someone grabs me, a bag is thrown over my head and my hands are tied behind my back. I believe they are doing the same to Michael, I can hear him yelp as they grab him. What is happening? One of my past activities has finally caught up to me. They pick me up and push me into the back of a car. Once I am in, they secure my feet my feet with what feels like a large zip tie, as they pull it tight around my ankle it pinches my skin a little. I feel another body pressing against mine, I hope that is Michael. It must be him, whoever it is, they are thrashing around trying to break free, but it's no use. We are secured and gagged, we're not going anywhere. This is not how I saw my night going a few minutes ago.

The car moves, I can feel the vibrations from the engine through my shoulder, pressed to the van floor. I try to pay attention to what I can hear and the turns we take, but it's hard to keep track. We have been driving for a few minutes when suddenly the vehicle stops. I hear two people get out and open the car door next to me. They grab my arm and pull me out of the vehicle, they leave Michael where he is and close the door behind me. They cut the zip tie around my ankles and lead me on a short walk, which crunches underfoot like some sort of gravel road for about 50 metres.

I feel the zip ties on my hands get cut as we stop. What is going to happen to me? Is this going to be the end? I am free to move though, I still have a chance. Suddenly, the bag over my head is pulled off. I squint at the sudden light, as my eyes adjust but after a few moments. A man in military uniform stands in front of me. It's General James from the competition. Oh crap, what is going on here? I guess they were not too happy I broke their network in front of everyone.

He looks at me and takes a few steps closer. 'Sam, I have been waiting for your call, it's been almost a week. I am not a patient man, you know.' I look around and see many of the same faces that were at the competition in his team.

I am not sure how I should respond but decide to just go with my usual tact or lack thereof, 'I can see that. You could have just called me to talk, you didn't need to kidnap me, you know.'

He nodded. 'You are probably right but the boys said you were getting a little frisky with your boy over there and they didn't want to watch where that was heading.' Oh wow, they have been watching me, watching me with Michael. Although it's dark, I can feel my cheeks get a little warm, I am blushing. Pull it together Sam. I have nothing to be ashamed of. 'I think it is time we had a proper talk, don't you?' He takes another step forward so he is right in front of me. 'You have some explaining to do, don't you?' he pauses for a moment and just looks at me waiting for me to respond but I don't say anything. 'My men will take you home now and Joe here will pick you up at 10 am. So we can have that chat, what do you say?' I consider it for a moment.

'Okay, but this time I can put myself in the car. No more snatch and grab. Deal?' The general agrees, with a slight smile creeping on to his face 'Done. I will see you tomorrow

Sam and you should consider toning down the public displays of affection, don't you think?' Wow, he had to go there, didn't he? I am almost dumbfounded and don't know what to say. Joe grabs my elbow and leads me back to the car, still a little aggressive, if you ask me 'Hey, watch it, bozo. No need to be so handsy, is there?' he just gives me a sharp look and squeezes my arm a little harder. I guess he does.

We get halfway back to the car and someone pulls the bag back over my head. Is that necessary? I roll my eyes even though I know no one can see it. They open the door as we approach the car and shove me back in next to Michael.

'Are you okay Michael?'

He murmurs something through his gag and then someone gives him a whack in the ribs just hard enough to stop him from saying anything further. The drive back seems to be faster than the initial one, maybe due to me knowing what is happening. I don't know if Michael will think the same though and I don't think I will be able to tell him what happened either. I will need to make something up to keep him out of this.

As the car comes to a halt, someone opens the door and pulls both of us out, throwing Michael onto the ground near his car and they lead me over to him. They hand me a pair of wire cutters.

'Don't remove your masks until you hear us leave. Understand?'

'Yes I understand,' I say. I hear them walk away and the car leaving. I wait a few more moments before reaching up and removing the bag from my head. I immediately untie Michael. I cut his legs free first and then his arms. He reaches up and pulls off the cloth bag over his head and gag in his mouth. 'What in hell was that? Who were those people? What have you gotten me involved in?'

I consider my answer for a few moments. 'They're a crime gang that wasn't happy with a job I did. Apparently I cost them a lot of money. They don't want me to do any more jobs for their competition and only do jobs for them' I hope my story is enough to satisfy his need to know what just happened. He looks angry and scared, but seems to accept the answer. He stands up and gets in the car.

'Let's get out of here,' he says. I can't argue with that sentiment and climb in.

Neither of us says anything on the drive home, but I can see he is thinking hard about something. I guess I'll find out soon enough. We pull up outside of my house and he turns off the car. I look over at him and wait. I think we both know we need to talk about what just happened. 'Sam, look I like you—' I go to respond but he cuts me off, '—I do, but this type of life isn't for me. I can't live my life thinking that someone could just grab me out of nowhere without warning. That isn't me. We had fun and I don't want to be enemies but I think we can't date anymore.' He pauses, I can see this is hard for him, he is fidgeting and looks extremely uncomfortable with the whole situation. He is gripping the steering wheel a little too tight and I can see him swallow slowly, trying to clear the lump in his throat. I don't think this is going to end well but I don't want to rush him or jump to any conclusions. I just wait for him to continue, 'I wish things were different.'

'You should really consider talking to the police about all of this, those people really seem like they aren't messing around. I know I am saying we shouldn't keep seeing each other but it doesn't mean I don't have feelings for you, I do. Just look after yourself Sam.'

I am not surprised. I knew this was a possibility; I can accept this. I look at him for a moment and then lean over, putting my hand behind his neck and pulling him toward me. He doesn't resist, and we kiss passionately for a moment. I pull back.

'Goodbye Michael'. I open my door. I get out and walk straight back to the house without looking back. I reach down to grab the handle when I feel a hand take mine. Michael pulls me back around towards him and pulls me back into his embrace, we kiss and instantly I feel the warm tingly sensation spread across my body like fire spreads across fuel. After a few minutes of lost time, the porch light comes on.

We both jolt back to reality and Michael catches his breath. 'Goodbye Sam.'

Is that it, are we still finished? I am so confused.

I reach for the door handle again, take a deep breath and head into the house. I can see Dad standing with his arms crossed to my right as I enter. 'You're late.' I face him and find my gaze fixated on his feet; if I look up, I might cry.

'I know Dad, I'm sorry.' he looks puzzled. Maybe he thought I would argue with him. 'If it's okay, can I just go to bed?' he must still be surprised.

'Okay, we can talk about this tomorrow night'. I nod and then turn for the stairs. What a night.

CHAUFFEUR

I WAKE TO THE SOUND of rain on our roof. It's a relaxing and sleepy kind of day, but my brain has been running wild most of the night. First, is that kiss with Michael on my porch before Dad ruined the moment. The feeling that pulsated through my body, I can almost feel it still moving through my nerve endings. It's a feeling I didn't know was possible, but if I am honest with myself, I loved it. It was like a drug pulsing through my veins, pure adrenalin. I want to feel it again, that much I know for sure. I don't know if last night was the end for Michael and me, I hope it isn't.

Or what about the fact that Michael and I essentially got snatched from outside the cinema last night by government goons? I don't even know how I should feel about that. It is the reason Michael doesn't want to continue whatever it is that we have going, but I enjoyed the adrenalin rush that I got from not knowing what was happening, thinking that it could be over. If I am honest with myself, it had similar electricity pulsing through my body as to when I was merging Michael's body with my own. I am not sure which one excited me more, which I enjoyed the most.

That reality is scary, I truly enjoyed being snatched up, having my life taken completely out of my hands. What kind of person does that make me, I shouldn't enjoy it, should I? I should be concerned about the meeting with the general today, but I am abuzz with the excitement of what could happen. The danger and possibility are exhilarating.

It's time to push both from my mind. I need to concentrate. Time to get out of bed and get ready for today. I push myself out of bed and head for the shower. I soak up the warmth as the water runs over my back and stay this way for a few minutes before I feel more relaxed and ready to face the day with a clear mind. I get out of the shower and head to my cupboard to pick out some clothes for the day, I better make sure that I wear something appropriate this time, I don't think last night's skirt was the best option to be snatched and thrown into the back of a government car or whoever else decides to snatch me today. Jeans and a shirt would be fine I think, maybe even a jacket to keep off the rain. Done and done.

I check the outfit in the mirror; I look good. I turn towards the door and start to make my way downstairs when I hear Dad talking on the phone with someone. It sounds important, but as soon as he sees me, he tells the person on the other end that he will call them back in a moment.

'Sam, I think we need to have a talk' he signals for me to sit at the dining room table. He follows suit and then pauses for a moment. I can see he is thinking hard about something, I just wait, whatever it is I will just take the punishment.

He looks up at me and holds my eyes 'About last night...' I figured that's what this talk was going to be about. I have never broken curfew before and I assume he will want to be tough on me to make sure I don't do it again.

'Okay, Dad.' His face is going a bit red now, he must be really mad at me.

'I think we should talk about how babies are made.' I blink. That wasn't what I expected him to say. He continues, scratching his chin and avoiding my eyes. 'I know it's a bit awkward talking to your silly old dad about these things but I need you to understand the risks about what you might be thinking of doing.' I feel my cheeks growing hot.

'Dad, we don't need to talk about the birds and the bees. I've had sex education at school, I know how it all works. Please stop, please stop talking.' I can feel myself starting to go even redder if that is possible.

'Sam, I know it's not something you want to talk to me about, but I saw how you and Michael were on the porch last night and I want you to be safe. I want you to know that even if it's awkward I am here for you to talk boys or whatever you need. Okay?'

'Dad, okay. I know I can talk to you about it, if I need to I will but please leave it for now, before I die of embarrassment.'

He shuffles in his seat. 'Do you think I want to talk about it either? Okay. I'll leave you be for now. I am heading to the office,. I will probably be late but please don't have Michael over when I am not here.' I nod, still a little thrown back by the topic of conversation. I was not ready for that.

The next hour goes past quickly and the conversation with Dad made me forget all about the other stuff. It is 10 am, the goons will be here soon to pick me up soon for my chat with the general. I grab my keys from the bowl and I walk out the front door, as I pull it closed behind me I see a reflection in the glass beside the door. It's that black SUV I have been seeing everywhere. It slows down as it approaches the front of my house and then comes to a complete stop. I take a deep breath and turn to face the car. The front window starts to go down and I see Joe looking out at me. It's been the Generals guys who were following me before the contest. They have been watching me for a while, oh crap maybe this meeting is not such a good idea.

I don't have much of a choice now. I will just go with it and hope for the best. I start to walk down the path and as I get close to the SUV, Joe gets out and opens the back door.

'Good morning Sam' As I look in the back seat, I see someone else sitting on the other side. It's a lady dressed like the other goons.

She hands me a black bag as I get in the car. 'You will need to put this over your head please. I believe you have worn one of these before?'

'Is this really necessary?' I ask and she lifts an expertly shaped brow.

'If you don't put it on voluntarily I can make you.' That's a bit aggressive. I shrug and do as I am asked, hearing Joe close the door next to me.

We drive for about 25 minutes before we stop. I can hear strange noises outside the car like we are in a wind tunnel or something. I feel the car jolt, like we're moving down. We must be in some sort of elevator. Eventually, I feel the car start to drive forward and then stop. I hear the guys in the front get out and one of them opens my door.

'You can take that off your head. We're here.'

GETTING THROUGH SECURITY

MY EYES TAKE A FEW moments to adjust after the headcover is removed, I look towards the door and slowly slide out of the SUV. We're in some sort of underground car park, it has fifteen or so black SUVs just like the one that picked me up. I continue to look around and all I can see is an elevator with a security pad on the left of the doors, which I assume is so only authorised people can enter the elevator. Joe gestures for me to make my way to the elevator and I do, but I notice something strange. There doesn't seem to be a way into this room I am in. How did we drive down here? Does one of these walls move out of the way? There doesn't seem to be a way in or out of this room except for the elevator doors in front of me and the SUV isn't fitting in there.

We walk up to the elevator door and the girl who was sitting next to me in the back seat walks up to the security pad and places her hand on the panel. A bright blue light flashes; it will be checking the palm print and also vein patterns. After a few moments the panel blinks green and she leans forward and a retinal scanner scans her right eye. The elevator door opens and she gestures me in. I step forward and make my way to the back edge of the elevator. It looks like any other building elevator I have been in, except it doesn't list the building floors. The girl enters and swipes what looks to be a security fob on a panel and it lights up with 10 level options that all say sub and a number randomly spread between sub 1 and sub 22. There must be at least 22 floors. She selects sub 4 on the panel and the doors close.

'Joe isn't coming with us?' The two guys stand by the SUV, expressions grim as the doors slide shut. I didn't expect a response but I wanted to break the awkward silence, unusual for me to be concerned about silence. I feel the elevator start to move downwards; oh we must be going underground.

'Joe is not authorised to enter the elevator,' she says. It takes only a few moments to arrive on our floor. As the doors open, I see a long hallway with several cameras on the ceiling. I am gestured to exit the elevator. 'This is where I leave you. Please make your way to the other end of the room and place your palm on the security pad at the other end.' I step forward and out into the long skinny room. I stop and look for a moment and then turn as I hear the elevator doors close behind me.

The walls are covered in a mix of different art and I can see looking around that there are a lot of sensors and cameras keeping watch on the room, probably the whole place. Where the hell am I? I hope I haven't made a mistake coming here, I hope this is not my final cell and I never leave. I shake the thought from my mind and take a deep breath. Pull yourself together, they're watching. At the other end of the room, I see the security panel and move toward it as instructed, looking at the artwork as I go. Once I reach it I pause for a moment before placing my hand on the panel as I had seen the girl do earlier. The same blue light scans my hand and after a few moments, a computer-generated voice requests I place my eye in front of the retinal scanner.

I stand there for a few moments while it scans my eye and it dawns on me; how do they have my palm print or my retinal scan information? Suddenly the computer-generated voice returns; *'temporary access authorised – Samantha Erkhart'*. The door opens in front of me and I see two guards standing holding what looks like machine guns at the back of the room, I enter and I can see that there are at least four more suitably armed guards around the room.

This looks like some sort of security checkpoint and as I step forward, one of the guards gestures for me to approach.

'Samantha, please place all of your personal items in the tray and remove all remaining metal objects.' I do as directed and I am gestured to walk into a machine in front of me. It's a full-body scanner. These people are not taking any chances. I am in the machine for what feels like five or six minutes before I am gestured to continue through. 'You will get your items back when you leave.' I don't see any point in arguing, it isn't likely to get me anywhere.

They gesture for me to go through the door in front of me, opening it for me as I approach. As I enter the next room, a pretty blonde girl who looks to be not much older than me approaches.

'We have been expecting you, Samantha, please follow me.' I follow her down a maze of passages and am amazed by how huge this place is. We finally get to a room that looks like a teenager's retreat, a big-screen TV, a wall full of movies and a selection of gaming consoles. 'Please, make yourself comfortable. The general is currently dealing with a situation and will be with you as soon as he has resolved it.'

She turns and closes the door behind her. Taking in my surroundings, I see multiple cameras watching the room, I jiggle the handle of the door experimentally. I am locked in. I guess I might as well make myself comfortable.

DOWN TIME

I DON'T KNOW EXACTLY how long I have been in this room. I don't have anything to tell the time, no clocks, no phones, they even kept my watch which is probably nearly as old as I am but I understand the need to ensure nothing is brought into a space like this, especially when you are dealing with a hacker. So, I am not annoyed by the fact that they took my stuff, I probably wouldn't trust me either.

Thankfully, the room is well supplied with entertainment options. Before long I have already watched *The Matrix* and nearly finished *Varsity Blues.* It must be close to three hours that I have been here. I hope the general doesn't keep me waiting here for too much longer. The movie wraps up and I begin to pace around the room, doing what a good hacker does and looking for vulnerabilities. I already considered using one of the gaming consoles to see what else is sitting on the network but I figured they probably wouldn't have given them internet access but if they did, it would be pretty restricted with what I could access.

I check out the cameras and see that they are all network-connected devices. I am sure I could manipulate them to gain some sort of advantage. Suddenly I hear someone unlock the door and the pretty blonde from earlier enters the room.

'Sorry for the delay. I have been instructed to get you some food as the general will be at least another hour. What takeaway food do you like? I will do my best to get it for you' Really another hour trapped in this glorified cell, it is essentially what it is. Yes, there are some things to keep me entertained and they are feeding me but in its basic sense, it is a holding cell to ensure they know exactly where I am and what I am doing.

Does he even have anything important to take care of or is this all some sort of power play, a way of me accepting that he is in charge here and that I have no control of what is happening. Should I protest at the extended wait and ask to leave? It probably wouldn't do me any good, it might make me feel better though. Well at least they are going to feed me, I am getting hungry.

'I would love some sort of chicken and chips with a coke zero please' she nods and leaves the room, locking the door behind her again.

It's probably another twenty minutes before she returns with takeaway store style BBQ half chicken, a family size box of chips and two 600ml bottles of coke. 'There is a fridge over there in the corner under the bench if you would like to put the second drink in there for later.' Later? I am going to be here for a while. Great.

'Thank you for the food.' She nods. 'How long have you worked for the general?' I ask, picking up a chip. My tone is conversational, but I figure I might as well see what I can learn from her. Her eyes narrow, as though she is considering if there is any harm in answering my question.

'A couple of years, he is a great boss. I can't really say anything more than that though. You don't have clearance to know what or who we are yet.' I sigh and sit on the couch to eat my food. She takes that as her cue to leave. This time, she doesn't lock the door. Is that on purpose or just a lapse of judgement on her part.

I eat most of the food and feel a bit better with my whole situation. I wonder how far I would get if I left this room. I'd probably be lucky if I could reach the end of the hallway. I get up and slowly open the door. I pull it open a crack and peer into the open hallway.

'Do you need something Miss?'

I nearly jump out of my skin. I look to the left and then the right but I don't see anyone. Who in the hell is talking to me? Then I see the camera hanging from the roof above me rotate slightly. They must be communicating to me through it. 'Your handler will be back in a few minutes, please return to the room.' I scowl and go back into the room.

I get through another hour of *She's all that* before I hear the door open behind me, as I turn to look if the pretty blonde had returned, I see the General enter with an armful of documents. Here we go…

MY RAP SHEET

AS THE GENERAL WALKS into the room, he looks over at me and gives me a once over. He seems as though he is analysing me, trying to almost read my thoughts. 'I see you have been well looked after in my absence.' I just nod and he gestures for me to come to sit with him at the table. I walk around the table and take the seat directly across from the general. As I do, he places the folder of files he was carrying in front of him. The paper is a little worn and crinkled at the edge, like someone has been scouring through it for months or more.. He gestures to the other two who had entered the room after him and they quickly leave the room closing the door behind them.

I watch the general as he opens the folder to reveal a dossier, with a photo of me on the front page! Oh crap, that folder can't all be about me. There is no way that they have that much on me, I am careful. Well, I thought I was anyway. He continues to look over the first few pages for a few minutes while I watch in silence. I know he is trying to put me off-guard, make me slip up and lose my cool. I need to hold it together.

'As you can see, Samantha, we have been watching you for a while. Or should I say, Foresight. That's who you really are, isn't it?' Okay, I am screwed. That pile is really about me. I might be staying here for a long time, what will they say to Dad? Will I be in a strange unexplained accident? Will they tell him I am a criminal? No, he won't believe that. I hope this doesn't cause him any trouble. 'You weren't easy to find, but we are good at finding out who people are.' He waits to see if I'll react but I don't, I just sit looking over at him. I am keeping this together, I have to.

'If I am honest Sam, can I call you Sam?'

I nod. 'Sam is fine.'

He smiles and appears to relax a little. leaning back in his chair and relaxing his shoulders. 'I don't think we can truly pin any of this on you. It could only be you. No one else can do what you do without a single trace. Most of the time, it's like it didn't happen at all. Half of my team has been trying to figure out your identity for years. It was just luck that gave us a hint in your direction.' Even if they know I am Foresight, at least they can't pin any of this on me. If I don't share anything incriminating, I might get out of this yet.

'I am glad you accepted our offer to attend the competition. It confirmed for me that it was you who we were looking for.'

'What do you mean your offer to the competition?' he almost laughs.

'Do you really think your vice principal was behind that? We brought to her attention some of the extracurricular activities you had been doing for other students and advised her that she should strongly recommend that you attend on the school's behalf. She wasn't completely sold on the idea, but I bet she will be impressed by all the new equipment that you won the school. You can't forget all the publicity of your win, either.'

That was a clever move. I should have been more careful. 'We had to do something to get a closer look at your skills, you were noticing our tails and we weren't getting anywhere with the surveillance anyway.' He closed the folder and leaned forward. 'Look, Sam, we both know that you are a very talented hacker. You have been using your skills mostly to take down drug and trafficking rings all over the globe and no one in the hacker community has a clue who you are. That in itself is almost unheard of, not one of them knows your true identity'. I fight back a grin. I can't show my hand; the risk is too high.

'I didn't bring you here to talk about all of that, honestly you have saved us a lot of work and brought pain to many organisations that we would love to bring down completely. You have been able to do it without all of the red tape and oversight we need to operate in. I think we can say I won't be recommending we pursue the hacker Foresight. It's a dead-end case with no clear links to anyone.' I nod and he continues. 'What I want to do is talk to you about a job, I have been tracking a hacker for months now and we can't even get close to them. The only person I know who I think could have any chance would be you.' He gestures at the camera and suddenly the two guys who left earlier at his behest come back through the door holding what looked to be another one of those manila folders, not quite as thick as mine and a laptop. They put it down in front of me before turning around and exiting the room again.

'I want you to track them down, find out who they are and help me catch them. They are not like you, they don't use their gifts for good, they just wreak havoc on the politicians and officials of this country. I am sure you can appreciate the pressure I'm under to prevent that from continuing.'

'What do I get in return?' he smiles at my reply.

'How about I make this all disappear for starters and we can see about getting you a nice government-funded car as a surprise bonus prize for breaking the time records? Maybe something fast? What about one of those nice new V8 mustangs everyone is drooling over these days, your choice of colour? I could even ensure that some very fruitful government building contracts land in your fathers favour, ensure his company is well looked after?'

That is a pretty sweet deal, is it a trap though? I guess I don't have much of a choice. 'How long do I have?' I ask and he looks very happy with my response. A wide smile creeps across his face and a sort of sparkle in his eyes.

'How long do you need?' I consider it.

'Give me a couple of hours and we can go from there.' He nods. 'I will need some more refreshments and maybe some snakes. The sugar will help me work faster.' He nods again.

'Consider it done. I will leave you to it. I will assume everything will be to your satisfaction with the equipment but if you need anything else just gesture to the camera and one of my team will get you what you need.' I nod and open up the computer to check out today's new toy. It looks suitable.

I flick through the dossier they have and it's very vague, but I can see some solid bread crumbs to start me off. This shouldn't be too difficult. I have to be careful not to reveal too much. I start by setting up the machine to hide my tracks. I'd rather not give myself away to my opponent, or let them know that I am hunting them. I am sure my benefactor, the General will be tracking my every move too, so I shouldn't make this too easy for them.

I start to search for traces through the deep web. They are pretty active on the marketplaces selling their stolen secrets. It only takes about an hour before I find a post that looks very similar to the target but by an account linked to an individual. I think they made a mistake, that's all I need. I track the account and find the alias which they are using in the real world. Gotcha.

I gather as much information as I can about them and put it all together in a nice little file on the laptop for the general's team. I can do better than this. Closing my eyes, I focus on my target and get to work. I target his accounts on every cloud platform, email addresses, even his uber account. I have access to everything. I glance over at the time in the bottom right corner and it's been a little over an hour.

Do I admit that I have finished? Or do I have a little fun and see what I can find out about the network I am on or the General? The answer is clear, I have to target the General, I have to know what I am up against and I need to flex my cyber muscles here a little so he really knows who they are dealing with if they don't already.

THE JOB OFFER

⊟

I FINISH WRAPPING UP the details of the target into a neat little package with some bonus details I dug up on my friend, General James. It was sadly very easy to break into his accounts. I even have access to his bank account, he used the same password for his social media accounts and his bank, with just with a few numbers changed at the start. Not very secure, James. You really need to do better.

I've have had my fun. It's time to call this thing a day, claim my new car and hopefully my freedom. It's an easy way to get that new car I wanted without trying to explain where I got the money to buy it. I am not sure if I need a Mustang but there is definitely worse cars out there I could get, especially when its free. Dad will love it though, that I know for sure.

It is almost 4 pm and Dad will be finishing up work in an hour or so. I look up at one of the many cameras watching me and gestured for them to come in. A few moments later the door opens and the familiar girl who had been waiting on me was back. 'Do you need anything?' I close the laptop and gesture for her to take it.

'I'm done. Tell James that I have put everything he needs in a folder on the desktop.' She looks surprised at my statement, obviously as she is staring at me with her mouth forming a small 'o' shape but after a few moments she straightens up, pulls herself together, picks up the laptop and folder on the table before exiting through the door she came through.

It would have to be at least another 30 minutes before I hear someone at the door. As it opens, I see the general come back through with a big smile on his face.

'I thought you were just yanking my chain when you indicated you would just need a couple of hours. You did it. You did what we have been trying to do for over a year now. That wasn't even two hours.' I just smile and decide this is probably my best time to mention my other activities.

'James, do you mind if I call you James?'

He shakes his head. 'That's fine.'

I gather my thoughts. I need to say this right to get the best effect. 'James, I think you need to pay more attention to your overdue bills. You had quite a few that hadn't been paid. I've fixed them all up and scheduled some automatic payments for you.' James looks a little confused now.

'Sorry, I don't think I understand, what do you mean?'

I smile now and continue, 'I was bored, so I decided to check you out. I have access to your private emails, social media and your bank accounts. If you don't mind me saying so, you do alright out of this gig of yours.' His facial expression changes, the casual smile is replaced with a stern cold expression, he gestures for someone and the door opens behind him. He whispers something and they disappear. He walks over to the fridge and takes out one of the cokes I was brought.

'You shouldn't have done that Sam.' If I am honest, he's right. Now I've poked the bear, I guess I can kiss the deal goodbye now. I might have to get used to a little less of these creature comforts I am being given. So stupid, I should have just done what I was asked, now I have probably gotten my self in a world of trouble. Stupid. Why do I do these things to myself.

A few minutes go by before the guy returns to whisper something in James's ear. He smiles at whatever they tell him, but returns to a stern look when he turns back to face me. 'Sam, Sam, Sam. That was a little foolish but I am not going to get worked up by you breaking into my systems, my team tells me you probably saved me some money in late fees, so I guess I should thank you.' He looks at me for a few moments before he softens a little. 'If you do that again in the future my response will not be as generous.'

I breathe a little easier at that comment. 'So can I leave now?'

He shrugs. 'Yes I guess you can but first, what colour do you want the car to be?'

'Dark blue definitely, any chance it could be a convertible?'

James shakes his head slightly at that 'I will see what I can do.' He gestures for me to take a seat.

I do as he asks and find myself sitting at the table across from him again. 'I want to offer you a job, Sam. You did in a few hours what none of my team could do. That is some impressive work. My team are some of the best in their field and you wiped the floor with them like they were toddlers playing with their parent's laptops. I didn't think that would have been possible, but every time I see your work, you surprise me with your skill. I want you on my team and I am willing to ignore certain indiscretions in your past. I think you could make a huge impact on what we are trying to do for our country.' He gestures to the camera again and one of his team enters with an envelope.

'Is everything ready?' he asks and they nod. He takes the envelope and slides it over the table to me. 'You will find a very impressive offer in that envelope Sam, one that doesn't normally come from a government job. I had to call in a favour to get this to happen.' I take the envelope and go to open it but he gestures for me to stop. 'Take it with you, I am told your dad is finishing work and about to start heading home. We wouldn't want him to get concerned about you, would we?' They are watching my dad as well. How long has this been happening in front of me and I didn't even know? I probably should have some sort of reaction to that information, I should be angry or annoyed or something, but I'm not.

He gestures for one of his team to come over 'please take Sam home.' His head is tilted as he watches me rise from the table, envelope in hand. 'I will expect an answer from you in a few days Sam. Don't keep me waiting.' I swallow and nod, leaving the room with his team member. As we reach the door, the General calls to me. 'Oh, and Sam?' I hesitate, my heart thumping. What if he's changed his mind and I can't actually go home? He continues. 'I expect all of my accounts to stay untouched and your access to disappear, if you get my drift. I wouldn't want anything like that to cause a strain on our relationship.'

I nod. 'Of course, consider it already done. Like I was never there.'

James smiles and waves his hand in dismissal. 'Enjoy the rest of your evening Sam.'

I go through another ride home with the bag over my head and before I know it the car is pulling up in front of my house. The bag is removed and the door is opened for me to exit the car. I let my eyes adjust and turn to see the now-familiar black SUV head off down my street. What a day!

MEET THE PARENTS

IT HAS BEEN A FEW WEEKS since my strange meeting with the general. The days seem to go past with ease. I have kept my head down as best I can but it's not so easy with all of the buzz about my big win at the security event. All the teachers are being super nice, it probably has something to do with all of the new equipment that turned up last week. New machines for the computer labs and many of the teachers got new laptops and it is all because of me.

Michael and I have crossed paths a few times, but all we seem to do is have extended stares before one breaks it off awkwardly. I think that relationship is toast but I don't think I blame him. It is not normal to be snatched in the middle of a date and thrown into a van. Well, not for most people, anyway.

I seem to have some sort of rockstar status with most students. Word of my annihilation of the other teams and for giving the operators of the hacking competition a bit of an uppercut is spreading like wildfire. I keep getting random strangers high fiving me and saying things like 'you go girl' or 'you rock'. I honestly hope this dies down soon, as I prefer my invisibility, just blending in with the crowd, but I won't hold my breath.

I am watch the clock tick over, waiting for the last few minutes of class to go by so I can get out of here. Finally, it rings. I quickly pack my things up and swing my bag over my shoulder and make my normal route out of school and towards home. I glance around, keeping a lookout for the familiar SUV but I don't see it anywhere. Maybe James will leave me to just decide on his offer. I have to admit the deal is pretty good, I checked up on analyst salaries in the Australian Signals Directorate, ASD for short and what they are offering me is three times that.

Do I want to work for the 'man' though? I just don't know if it's me. I will have to figure it out soon though, James doesn't seem like he would be the most patient person and it's already been more than a few days. I don't want to keep him waiting. But, if I say no, will that send my deal out the window? I don't want to be the target of investigation for previous events. I can't let the potential danger sway my decision though, I need to want this, not just do it so I don't end up in jail.

I turn the corner near my house and I see it. HOLY CRAP. A shimmering blue convertible mustang parked in my driveway. James delivered on his promise, my additional prize has arrived. I pick up the pace and just stop short of the, oh I don't know what it is but it's mine. It really is mine, that's if Dad lets me keep it. He has to let me keep it, it's a prize that I earnt and he is proud of my achievement. I won't worry about that right now; I will just enjoy this moment.

After a few moments, I come back down to earth and notice Dad's ute parked up beside the house. He's home early. I'll assume he already knows about our new toy and hopefully, he has the keys so I can give this thing a test drive. I turn and head to the front door and as I walk through, I hear Dad's voice, talking to someone. Maybe he is on the phone. I'll just go in and let him finish. As I round the corner through to the lounge room, I see Dad and General James, sitting in the chair across from him. I stop in my tracks, taken back by his presence, in my home, of all places. I was not expecting that.

As Dad sees me he beckons me to come over. I do as asked and sit down next to him. 'Sam, we have been waiting for you. General James is from the Government group who sponsored the competition you participated in a few weeks ago. He tells me that his bosses were very impressed by your efforts at the competition and decided to award you something a little special for your efforts. You may have noticed it on your way in, the blue mustang.' I have to pretend that this is a surprise to me as I shouldn't know about it.

'That is mine?! Seriously, that's mine? I don't know what to say. Thank you so much.' James reaches into his jacket pocket, retrieves the keys and tosses them to me. 'You're welcome Sam, your skills were very impressive.'

Dad has a huge grin on his face, 'I am proud of you, so proud.' I think I start to blush slightly with all this attention. 'You'll have to let me take it for a drive, now and then.' I smile, he is letting me keep it. Getting to school from now on is going to be much easier, that's for sure.

'Sam, the general here wants to discuss an opportunity with you, one that will have you go work for the government and also fund university if you would like to work part-time while studying. They will cover everything. I think it sounds like a great opportunity.' He looks at James for a moment and then turns back to me. 'How about I give you two a few minutes to discuss. If you need anything let me know Sam.' He looks back at James. 'It was great meeting you General' he rises to his feet and they shake hands. Dad turns and leaves the room, allowing us to talk in private.

'I hadn't heard from you. I was getting worried. I am starting to think you don't like us.' He has a strange smile on his face, kind of a joking smile. Not a side I had seen of him before, I drop my eyes to the car keys in my hands. The General notices where my attention has drifted. 'As promised, your reward for a job well done. Do you approve?'

'Yes, I am very happy. Thank you.'

'Good. Now, let us get down to business. Do you accept my offer?' I don't know what I want to do yet, I think it's a great option but this isn't a path I had seen for myself. I need more time.

'James, look, I think your offer is really good but I need more time to decide.' He looks at me for a few seconds before chuckling.

'Do I need to offer you more money? Will that convince you? Some perks, travel? What is it going to take to get you onboard?' I feel a little awkward at that statement, I don't know what I want or what will make me decide right now on the offer.

'Honestly, I just need more time to think it through. That's all. Can I just have 'till the end of the week?' James looks at me, his mouth a stern line. It must be frustrating for a General like him, to have to try to hard to recruit a 17-year-old.

'I will give you four days.'

He gets up from his chair and steps closer to me 'Sam, this is a great offer. Make sure you give it full consideration. You have four days, that's it. If I haven't heard from you by the end of the fourth day, I will take it as a no.'

I hold his gaze for a moment. 'Four days. You will have your answer in four days.' He turns and starts to walk out of my house but stops just short of the front door.

'We found your guy, by the way, the one you helped us identify. We could use your help to find out more about him, help with building a true dossier. Maybe it can be your first assignment.' He turns and walks through the front door.

He is good, I want to know more, I want to dig deeper and chase down the threads just sitting there waiting for someone to pull them. He understands me well. Well played General James, well played.

THE DECISION

IT'S BEEN THREE DAYS since I had a surprise visit from the General and I can feel that looming deadline hanging over me inching closer by the minute. It is always on my mind. I can't concentrate on much else without it drifting back in. I just need to make a decision. I need to get it done; seriously can it really be that hard?

I am out driving in the car with dad, he really loves this thing. He takes every opportunity to take it for a drive. It's been good to just hang out and enjoy something nice like this together.

'Sam, can you tell me what you would like for dinner? Sam? Earth to Sam.' Whoops, I must have zoned out again. 'Sorry Dad, what was the question?' he just looked at me a little confused and although he was trying to hide it, a little annoyed with me as well. 'What do you want for dinner Sam?'

'What about Chinese? Or maybe we could go to that awesome pizzeria we used to go to when I was little? The one that has those amazing garlic pizzas.'

Dad smiles. 'We haven't done that in forever. You must be feeling a little nostalgic. Why not, let's just do it.'

At the next set of lights, Dad does a U-Turn and pointed us back towards our new dinner location, a trip down memory lane. We drove the twenty-minute trip in silence, although I did see Dad look over at me a few times. He looked like he wanted to say something, but was working up the courage. He probably wants to know the million-dollar question – have I made a decision? We arrive at the pizzeria and make our way in. It looks the same as I remember it. The couple who run the place look a little older, but it has been years since I have been here. Dad asks for a table for two and is directed over to an old dinner style booth in the back. We both slide on in and take our menus from the table.

After a few minutes, the waiter returns to take our order and gets us some drinks. As soon as she leaves, Dad clears his throat. I guess he has decided now is a good time to discuss whatever it is that he wanted to talk about. I look up and see that he has that serious dad face on that he does when he wants to be all serious with me or would like to get up me for something. Maybe he doesn't want to talk about the job offer from the general.

'Sam, I want to ask you a question, and I want you to be honest with me. Okay?' What the hell does he want to ask me? What have I done or should I have done, that is making him get all serious?

'Sure, Dad what do you want to know?' he looks down at his drink, I assume figuring out how to say whatever this is he wants to ask me.

'These skills you have with the computer that the government is interested in and that won you the competition as well as that sweet ride we came to dinner in... I get that I don't understand them completely, but I know the attention you are getting and how easy you won the competition. I know it was easy for you, the general told me that he has never seen someone with your abilities. How did you get so good at computers?' he looks me straight in the eyes and holds my gaze. 'Skills like these would need to be practised and honed to be as good as you. Is that true?'

I fiddle with my own drink, pushing the ice cubes around with my straw. 'Yes. I guess that's correct'.

'So, have you been doing anything that would get us in trouble? Like with the law, get you locked up?' I take a sip of my coke; I seem to suddenly have a very dry mouth.

'Dad, look. I would like to be able to say I haven't done anything illegal, but I can't. I have been doing things, for a few years now. Nothing that has been for my advantage, just hurting bad people a little.' I look over at Dad and he has gone a pale colour. I better put him at ease somehow. 'Dad, I am very good at this stuff and I was very careful to stay hidden. Nothing will come back on either of us, nothing.' He seems to relax a little with that, but not much.

'Do I want to know what sort of stuff or is this one of those situations when it is better ifI just don't know what has happened?' I nod and he seems to take that as his answer. 'I assume that is why the government people have suddenly come into our lives. Should I be worried about the general?' Should Dad be worried? Should I be worried about the General and his secret army? That's a good question, one I know the answer to.

'No, you don't need to worry about James. He just wants me to come work for them, use my skills to help them take down the worst of the worst. I just don't know if it's what I want to do. I think it's a great offer where I can still do university and have it all paid for while also working for James' team.'

He raises his eyebrow at me, 'James? Not General?' Oh, I didn't even notice I did that.

'Yes, James. He told me to call him James, not General.'

The pizza arrives and we eat with some minor chatter. The garlic pizza is so amazing, I think it may be better than I remember, if that is possible.

'Can I ask you another question?' I nod and he continues, 'This job will allow you to use your skills for good, you will be paid very well and you will get to do what you love without any threat of going to jail for it. Do I have that about right?' I smile, it is that simple, isn't it? It really is.

'Yeah, I guess so.' Give it to Dad for making something so complicated as deciding my future so simple.

'Does that mean you have made your decision? Are you going to work for James?' I consider the question for a minute, take a sip of my drink.

'I guess. It looks like I will be going to work for the government. Helping them fight the good fight.' I look at Dad and I think he likes the answer, he has a big smile on his face. The waiter comes back and collects our plates and leaves the bill for us. Dad gets up and gestures for me to follow. He walks to the counter and pays our bill.

As we walk out the door, he looks over to me. 'I think I should drive home again, that way you can tell the general you have made your decision.' He has a bigger smile on his face. I think he really loves my new car. I nod and get in the passenger side. I put on my seat belt and reach into my pocket for my phone.

I open a new message thread for James and type just two words: *I'm in.* I hope I have made the right choice.

It took only a few seconds to get a response: *Great to hear. We will be in touch very soon.*

THE SURPRISE

⊡

IT'S A LITTLE STRANGE TODAY, everything seems to have a weird brightness or vibrancy. I know it is because my mind is abuzz because I meet with James today. It's the only explanation or maybe Dad slipped something into my morning coffee, would he? No, that's a silly thought. I am dressed a little nicer today than my first visit, a bit more business-like. If I am going to be working for them, I should make a little effort to look presentable. It's not like I didn't have the time. I've been up for hours.

It was all arranged a few days after I texted James, I would finish school and today I would start my new job. The time has gone by fast; the whole situation still feels a bit surreal if I am honest. I am just sitting out here on the front stairs waiting for my ride to get here, my usual black SUV. I haven't seen them around in months.

I can't believe school is over and I am joining the government offensive cyber unit or whatever they are officially or unofficially. Who really knows? I will be probably listed as a secretary or IT support officer officially. No one will know what I do except the team I work in that's how this all works. We don't exist and don't share anything with anyone else.

I see the SUV come around the corner and pull up in front of my house.

The driver rolls down his window and as I approach says, 'Get in the back'. I nod and open the back door to climb in. No one else is in the back seat waiting for me this time, just the driver and myself, it would appear. I climb in and fasten my seatbelt. I look around for the usual headcover but don't see it anywhere.

'Sorry, I don't see the headcover. Do I need to wear one?' I see his eyes connect with mine in the revision mirror.

'No, there won't be any need for that. James has authorised you to go in un-blinded. He said you are now one of us.'

I settle in for the drive, I remember it was pretty short. It really shouldn't take too long. We start to drive towards the main part of town, I wonder where the office is located. It's probably in a shady old abandoned-looking warehouse or something like that. Maybe it is just a boring office building hiding in plain sight. That's more likely. We keep driving and suddenly we enter a car wash. What are we doing here? The SUV looked pretty clean when I got in. the driver made his way through to an automatic car wash towards the back of the facility. Another car is just entering the car wash, so we wait in line behind it. The car goes in and the doors all close around it. I can't see anything, but I can hear the brushes and the high-pressure water jets cleaning the car.

We sit there for about five minutes before the noise stops and a few moments later the doors open, allowing the car to drive out the other end all clean and dry. It looks like the machine does a pretty good job. The driver roles the car forward and rolls down his window to use the machine, which allows you to select the type of wash cycle you want. He pulls out a security fob and waives it in front of the unit after selecting the premium wash. The agency must have an account, I will have to get myself one of those fobs to keep the mustang clean. The machine makes a strange noise and the main screen slides down revealing a new screen behind it, the driver enters some sort of code and says, 'Let's dive down the rabbit hole.' He looks at me in the mirror now and I can see he has a smile on his face.

'Code accepted' comes from the machine and the screen slides back to its original place. He rolls forward and enters the car wash just as the car before us did. What the hell is going to happen in here? I knew something was weird when I came blindfolded but this is just crazy. The doors close on both sides of the machine and the water starts spraying just like any other car wash but it doesn't come over to the car, something starts to move though—this is a hidden lift, we are going down to a hidden underground car park. How did they build all of this without anyone knowing? I guess people knew, just not people like me, the clueless people who drive past this place almost every day without any idea this place was here.

It only takes a few moments and the car comes to a stop. This room looks familiar; this is where they removed the blindfold the first time. The elevator is in front of me and as with the first visit, the driver doesn't get out. 'This is where I leave you. Please exit the vehicle and Kate over there will help you.'

I climb out and a woman who must be Kate meets me with a smile, 'welcome Sam. The General is waiting for you downstairs.' As I enter the elevator, I see the SUV start to go back up in the lift, it makes sense that the car would have to leave pretty quickly, it would be a little weird if the car wash finished and no car came out the other end.

Would anyone notice though? Probably not. I have never noticed this car wash before and I have been coming past this place for years. I like to think I'm an observant person but I missed this place completely. Whoever built this subterranean monster knew what they were doing. I feel like I am just dreaming and I am waiting to still wake up.

The doors to the lift close. This is it, I am heading down to sign away my rights and join the hit squad. Oh, I can't wait. This is going to be fun.

WEEK ONE

MY FIRST WEEK is nearly over. I've been doing nothing but grunt work all week. Honestly, I think the rest of the team doesn't like me very much. It is only a small team of around 20 people, although I don't really know exactly how many people work for James, just the team they have assigned me to. There could be hundreds of people hiding out in this weird underground fortress, it's huge that I know for sure but I only have limited access, my fob doesn't work for most doors except the room I work in and the lounge room I was stuck in for hours the first time I was brought here. It is not so bad though. It has a comfy couch and the fridge is always fully stocked with goodies which I have utilised several times already.

It's not like I can just duck out and get myself a cheeseburger or anything. Once you are in you, stay in, or at least until my ride comes back for me anyway. I still can't get my head around the awesome car wash entrance. I am not allowed to bring the mustang to work. It's too conspicuous and I can't argue with their logic. I am one of a very few in my team who gets chauffeured. I like it though, actually makes me feel important. No one else here thinks so. I am at the bottom of the food chain, the bosses pet project that got an easy ride in. No one likes me and no one, except for James it seems, wants me here.

I am the outcast, the black sheep of the group who, as far as the rest of the team goes, does not belong here, doesn't deserve to be here and I think they intend to ride me until I quit. I don't blame them for not wanting me here. Most of them have multiple degrees, have worked their ways through multiple mundane positions in government to get an opportunity to be part of this secret group, and here I am just wandering on through the door at James' behest without proving myself first. I get it.

I am literally making myself stupider with this job though. I am doing DNS searches and checking through log files. The grunt work you would give a trained monkey to do for you. The only thing that entertains me a little is I get to monitor chatter on the dark web. Keep an ear on the ground for something suspicious or even remotely problematic that the team should know about. I am just a paid intern though, well that's how it feels anyway.

It's Friday and I am so ready to finish up my first week of this, whatever it is I'm doing here. At least I am getting paid well and hopefully if I bide my time, the team will trust me a little. Just need to keep doing as I am told, get coffee, get lunch and any other leg work that is needed. I'll get my shot and I just need to grab it by the horns when I do.

'Sam, can you please come over here? I need you to look at something for me.' That's Gabby, she is a pretty cold and hard woman. I think she is early 40s maybe and is probably the only one that is not giving me shit, or riding me all the time. I like her, I think she is pretty good behind the keyboard from what I have seen. She has been in the trenches for a while and you can tell she's an old school hacker, an 80s movie stereotype. I better see what it is she wants me to look at, probably more grunt work or something she doesn't want to do. She hasn't done it to me before though, maybe she has something interesting for me to do. I can only hope.

I walk over and stand by her desk until she looks up from her screen. 'James thinks you have some special skills. He thinks you could be the best of all of us. What do you say to that?' She looks at me waiting for a response but I don't give one, I just hold her gaze and she sighs, continuing, 'I don't know about all that, but I am willing to give anything a go. Look, I've hit a wall on a suspect I have been trying to chase for a few days and I know you found that guy for James in a few hours. I figured you might be able to help and I can see what you are capable of…'

She's testing me. I am not even sure she needs my help with this but it's an in with her and I want to stop doing DNS scrapping.

'Okay, what do you need?' She points at some information on her screen. I look over it and it is some details for a target and she writes down the case file number on a piece of paper: *646IN9*. She hands it to me.

'I need you to work your magic on this suspect, tell me if they are responsible for the recent large money transfer into their bank account. Is it stolen? Is it proceeds of crime?

Anything you can find out, get it back to me by the end of the day.'

Well, that should make my day a little more interesting. I have almost four hours left on my shift and that is way more than I will need. I just nod to Gabby and turn back towards my desk. I sit down at the machine and look around my desk for a moment. This is it, this is my way off the shit list. I need to bring my A-game. I get back up and head for some supplies. I am going to need some snacks, some sugar and carbs to burn off. I get an assortment from the lounge and sit back at my desk to get to work.

I log in and let my fingers run over the keyboard. I let my gifts control my flow, I can feel what I need to do and just start doing it. I run through years of information on this guy. He is nothing, he is no one at all. How did he get 3 million suddenly appear in his bank account? I double down and troll through the deep web for any data on this guy. Who is he, really? Is what he is letting us see the real him or is that just a cover for something or someone more sinister?

I finish off my fourth coffee and a packet of plain potato chips. I am getting nowhere. I can't see anything. He is clean but is he too clean. Then I stumble across a recent court filing with his name on it. This is a will from this guy's grandmother, she was sitting on a bit of a nest egg it would seem. This guy got one of those scam contacts, you know the ones where they say we have inherited a bunch of cash and we need to contact them to get it. This one is probably the only one that is real in all of Australia, no scrap that, the world.

I will need to verify this, but I think this guy is actually on the up and up. I double-check everything and my opinion is confirmed. He is legit and inherited the large sum. I collect all of the evidence and attach it to the case file, as is the protocol. When I do, Gabby looks over at me. 'You've finished already? Let's see what you put together.' She looks over the files and my notes and shoots me an approving glance. 'Well done Sam.'

I hope that means I am done with the grunt work. I guess I will find out soon. What is next? 'Do you need me to help you with anything else Gabby?' she taps her fingers along the file I put together and looks like she is considering my request, 'actually I do have something you might be able to help me with. Let me get authorisation first. It is above your current clearance.' She gets up and heads out the door.

I don't see Gabby again before my shift finished. I'm guessing something came up. I gathered up my things and headed out for my ride, which was entering the car park as the elevator doors open. As I start to walk to the SUV, I notice it isn't empty. The driver gets out of the vehicle and opened the rear door. It's Gabby.

'See you on Monday Sam. I'll have something for you then'. She walks past me and into the still open elevator, I watch as she turns back to face me and the elevator doors close between us.

What was that all about? I wonder what she has for me. It sounds juicy though if she needed to get authorisation for me to even look at it. I shrug it off and get in the SUV, it's movie night with Dad. Time to get home.

THE MARK

IT IS MONDAY MORNING and I am in the lift on the way down to the office. I can't hide my excitement even if I tried. I've been going over this in my mind all weekend. What is Gabby going to give me? Is it going to be my first real case? I hope it's a way to make my mark and prove to the rest of the team that I have value. I know I can do this job and I can do it well. I just need them to believe that.

I arrive on my floor, which honestly, I don't even know what level it is on. I just swipe my fob on the panel outside the elevator and it just takes me down to this level. It takes at least 30 seconds to get to this floor so I calculate somewhere over ten floors below the surface, but I am just guessing. The doors open and I exit, turning left as normal. Taking the long hallway past several other rooms and the lounge before I get to my room.

I place my hand on the palm scanner and wait for it to request my access code. I enter it and walk through the door. Gabby sees me enter the room and beckons me over. I try to calm myself, I don't want to look like I am too excited. I need to act cool now. I arrive at her desk and she gestures for me to pull up a chair.

'Sam, I want to go over the job I have for you. I need you to understand this is a very important job that I am about to give you and this could blow back on me if you screw it up. So don't screw it up, okay?' I just nod a little too aggressively, letting a bit of my excitement come through. 'This job will make the test case you did to get in here look like nothing. This person, whoever they are, is a ghost. They leave no traces; they have no ties to anything in the real world. They remind me of you a little. The only thing we have is a style, a sort of way they do things.' She pauses there and turns to grab a box from beside her desk and places it in front of me on the desk. 'that is just a part of what we have. The case file is on the top of the box.' She grabs the arm of my chair and turns it so that I am facing her.

'I need your best work on this Sam. I need you to give me everything you have. I need you to be a ghost just like him, just like I know you can be. To find this hacker, whoever it is, I need you to go dark, use those gifts I have been hearing so much about but if you find something, I need them to be unaware we are on to them or they will vanish like they were never there at all. James has authorised you full access to these files and has instructed the team that this is your case now, this is your only job until you find them.'

Wow, this is big. Gabby is giving me a shot alright. This is the shot, the one that could make me a true member of this team. I take a deep breath and exhale slowly.

'I've got this. You can count on me.'

Gabby smiles at me. 'Then get to work kid, you have a ghost to hunt'. I smile at that comment, one of those real smiles that do more than just sit on your face but almost make your whole body illuminate from it. I turn and pick up the box and start to turn back to my desk. I stop though and turn back, 'Thank you Gabby, I appreciate you giving me this chance and I know you have probably put yourself at odds with the rest of the team to do it.' She shrugs, glancing around the room at the team and lowers her voice. 'Just prove me right. Shut them up by doing something else no one has ever come close to doing.'

At that, I get to work. I start by reading through everything in the box. Gabby was right, they are a ghost. They don't have anything at all on this hacker, they can't even really confirm or deny if any of the incidents that have been allocated as being one of theirs are actually them. The skill is impressive, to say the least, they leave no logs, no traces, nothing to say they had even been on a system at all except the missing millions of dollars or the fact that files had been leaked.

I wouldn't admit this to anyone else on the team, but I am impressed. They are an artist, a true Michelangelo of the hacker world. One I am thinking whose skills might surpass my own. Admitting that pinches a little. It is possible though. This mark might be tougher than I thought. I will not let that affect my resolve; I will find them. Somehow.

I log on to the systems and review the job files. There are even more potential hacks linking back to my mark but again nothing concrete, just analysts feeling as though this was them. Just that intuition and I am starting to get that same feeling for them, like they leave a scent behind that is just uniquely them. Like you can just feel their presence, but you just can't put your finger on why.

For days, I dredge through hundreds of hours of notes from analysts, from victim statements and collected images. Nothing at all that helps me. Just rumours and hearsay. Arrrrr I need to figure out how to approach this, how I can narrow my search. Maybe I need to forget all of these files and just do what I do best. Hunt. I get up from my desk and look around the room. I am alone. No one else is here. What time is it, oh no, it's 11 pm? Dad is going to be pissed at me, I am late again. This is the fourth night this week.

I gather up my stuff and call the security desk to request my ride home. 'It's already waiting for you Sam,' is the response. Maybe I am starting to make a habit of this if they are already prepared for my late departure. Time to get out of here.

THE SPIDERS WEB

IT'S A NEW WEEK. I'm sitting here staring at my screen trying to think about how I am going to do this. Then I realise that I am not going to get anywhere by just staring at the screen. I need to log in and get to work before anyone around here thinks they have made a mistake giving me this case. I close my eyes and just clear my mind of all the noise and then just get to work.

I start by scouring the dark web underground forums for any whisper of their activities. I even create a custom program in python to automate some of the chatter filtering to help me push off nonsense or just rumours. I continue this for several more days when I start to get hints of a potential hacker's name 'Shadow'. They are a recluse and barely touch the forums or market places.

I have something to go on now. It might turn out to be nothing, but it is all I have got right now. I do some adjustments to my python tool to look for anything to do with shadow. The data flows in, discussions, rumours, all just talk from other hackers and criminals who have crossed paths with this mythical creature. It is like they are some boogie man who creeps in the night to punish naughty children and scumbags alike. The chatter would make me believe they are a man but I have nothing to prove that. They are truly feared, that is for certain. Anyone who has crossed them or tried to winds up with some serious heat on their tail, all their secrets laid bare and not a penny left to hide.

I get the feeling that they don't like anyone talking about them, as any conversation is quickly stopped with no explanation. Maybe they receive a warning shot and if they don't stand down will receive the wraith of 'Shadow'. It's a cool handle but I think my own is better. Foresight has a much cooler ring to it.

I start to put some pieces together. They've been active in some form for around 8-10 years that I can tell, maybe more or maybe a little less, it's hard to pin them down on anything that far back but if that is when they started that's where I need to focus. Maybe they slipped up some time, maybe they were just learning, feeling out the skills they had like I was back then. I narrow my lens to focus on that, digging deeper and deeper.

I can feel them starting to come together, painting a picture in my mind. They don't seem to want to hurt anyone. They go after thugs and criminals, same as I did. Mostly big rich hedge fund people who would walk over people not caring who they hurt to make a buck. He would take everything from them, but mostly money. If all of these victims are his, he must have a lot of money by now, but why does he keep doing it if that is the case?

I can see that they like to take down corrupt officials as well, he doesn't seem to go after the money on those occasions, just reveals any toxic behaviour, showing who they really are, thugs and lousy husbands or wives. Wow, I can see why they have a target on their backs, it seems they have truly aimed at some very powerful people all over the world.

I stumble on something new, a whisper of a new target, a lady who is profiting off taking people's homes after giving desperate victims untenable loans that would never be able to be covered. They are just whispers, to stay out of the way, not to get wrapped up in the fight. To stand down if she tries to get help from the dark underbelly of our world. She is truly on her own in this fight and it's one which almost everyone who resides down here already feels she had lost just by being his target.

Maybe I can use this to my advantage. If I dig into her life, follow her money and wait for a bread crumb to form. If I can be there when their money moves, if I am quick enough, I can follow it through to Shadow. I look over statements, purchases, sales everything. There has to be something, there has to be one mistake, one glimpse of who they are. I need to keep searching. This is my one shot to find him, I can't mess it up.

THE EPIPHANY

⊟

THE MONEY IS MOVING in small amounts to attempt to go unnoticed, hundreds of them. I put tags on the transactions and follow the weaving beauty of what is happening. Thousands of transactions moving through thousands of more transactions. It then comes together in a single account and as quickly as it hits, it moves again, but this time it jumps into bitcoin. It is going to get washed. Everyone does it. I have even done it, I am panicking a little now, I am going to lose the trail. No, No, NO!

It's gone. I must have missed something. I go back and look at everything again, but the money is gone. Except some of the money was siphoned off in the middle of the first frenzy of transfers, 10 million dollars brought together and then deposited into a charity. Maybe Shadow doesn't keep all of it, after all, maybe he is more of a robin hood than a thief. Maybe he is a good guy. It doesn't change anything though. He is my target and I need to stop messing around and just find them.

I look closer at the charity payment. It is done in the name of Global funds Group. I look at the organisation closer and it has one registered director — Timothy Peters. Who is Timothy Peters? He is a clean slate except he is listed as a director on more than 10 different organisations? I search for transactions to charities from these entities over the last 10 years and there are more than two hundred of them with a total of more than a billion dollars. This is crazy, this funding alone has probably kept the lights on for many of these charities. Letting them do what they do best and help people. Shadow is the reason many of them still operate.

He is clever. Then I spot something, an IP address for a local address. He couldn't be that stupid, could he? I dig deeper and one of the transactions was done at a local internet café. I check the café systems out. Maybe I can get a look and see if they have video cameras. I get through with default logins; it works too many times. I look and they still have footage from that day and time, so I pull it back to my machine to review. I can see only one person at the café using a computer and they are as old as my grandparents. I don't think it would be them. Then, in the back corner of the room, I see a young guy pull his phone from his pocket and click something on his screen while he is paying for his coffee. It runs some sort of quick script on the screen and disappears as fast as it comes up. If you were not looking, you would have missed it.

Is this him? He looks well built, athletic even. He has dark hair but he is looking in the wrong direction to see his face. He hands the server cash, but for some reason, the barrister appears to stop him and looks as though he asks for a different payment method. Maybe he didn't have enough change, so they pull out a wallet and takes a card. It's a MasterCard of some kind. I need to get that transaction data. I send up a request for details of that payment through official channels, although I could probably get it myself if I wanted. I impatiently pace as I wait for the information to come back.

It's a prepaid card, no way to trace it. Grrrrr. I need to find a way to get him. I am so close now. Focus Sam, focus, we can do this. There has to be something else I can use. Then I see it across the road in a distance. It's an ATM with someone using it as he walks out of the shop. Maybe it gets a glimpse of his face, it's a long shot, but it's all I have. I get access to the footage from the ATM, another dead end. He looks at his feet just as he walks out of the shop. He has done his research, he knows where everything is. He deserves the name Shadow. He is gone and I have lost my chance.

Then I see It, two girls across the street about 30 metres away from my mark are taking selfies. Looks like they are leaning into some flashy car. The camera would be facing him. I need to find out who those girls are and scrape their social feeds for something that could identify him. I get to work clearing up the image of the girls and start a facial recognition crawl on all the usual social media sites. It is running for hours, still nothing. I need to find them.

I distract myself by starting to put notes on the job, while it's fresh in my mind. I get about halfway through when I get a ding, a screen jumps up on my machine: *Match Found*. I feel some butterflies build in my stomach. I can get him, this is it. I crawl over the girl's posts and there it is, a shot right in front of me with his face visible, a bit blurry but I can clean it up. I run it through an optimiser with a focus on the figure in the background. I have it, I have his face.

I stop and breathe for a moment. Now I need to be smart about this, I can't let him know I am onto him, a gentle touch on this one. I put his face through our databases and I get a hit; he has a driver's licence. Jacob Loxley. I have an address. Loxley? Really, he couldn't do better than a Robin Hood reference. It is fitting though, I suppose. I gently gather further intel on him, finding out everything I could. I needed to make sure my report was flawless. It's time to catch my prey. It's been a long time coming and I don't want him getting loose on me.

Once it's done, I just look at the screen for a moment. I did it, I really did it. It has been three weeks since Gabby gave me this job. I was starting to have doubts I could get my mark. If I would capture my prey, but here it is, all wrapped up with a bow around it. I submit the case file with the updated tag: *ready for review – completed*. As I do, a few moments later I hear someone spit out a mouthful of coffee, it was Gabby. She must have been surprised by the alert. She quickly gets up and grabs something to dry the mess and then thinks twice halfway through and just throws the cloth on the desk.

She heads straight for me, throwing her arms around me and almost screams, 'you did it, No more doing coffee runs for you girl' You did it you really did it. You solved the unsolvable. You caught a ghost. The shadow of the dark web no one could even get close to. You did though.' I am finding it hard to breathe, she is squeezing me so tight, everyone is looking at the exchange now. They are all staring at me, I am getting a little awkward now.

Suddenly, she releases me. 'The General, we need to take this to the General now. We can't have him getting away. If he gets wind we have his identity he'll vanish.' She grabs my arm and yanks me in the direction of the door. I guess I am going to see the boss. We get to the elevator and Gabby swipes her fob as I normally would but she also touches a blank steel square panel just above the fob sensor. It appears to be a hidden button.

This place surprises me all the time. A few moments go past then a computerised voice comes out of some speakers in the control panel, 'please provide voice print and stand in front of the retinal scanner. The panel drops down revealing the retinal scanner and

Gabby lets it scan her eye before saying a strange poem verse. 'Ghosts have just as good a right. In every way, to fear the light, As Men to fear the dark.'

The computerised voice comes back over the speaker, 'Authorisation granted – secure area access'. The elevator jumps into motion, heading deeper into the earth and the panel closes. A few seconds go by and it comes to a stop with the doors opening in front of me. When we walk out a full body scan is initiated and the red light turns white, when it does a hidden door on the other side of the room opens up. Gabby opens her arms wide, 'Welcome to the General's office'.

We walk through the door and I can see I very masculine styled room with dark timber furniture, a couple of big leather couches like you would see in a fancy gentlemen's club or something. One wall has some sort of virtual scenery with an amazing view of a cityscape at night. This is a lovely office, I guess it pays to be the boss.

The general looks up at us as we enter. 'You better have a good reason for bringing Sam down here without authorisation Gabby.' She looks a bit sheepish at that statement and then just shrugs it off.

'We have something for you, the whale we have been chasing. Sam here landed it solo.'

A smile comes over his face, 'Show me, show me what you have'.

Gabby turns to the scenery wall, 'showcase 3981TH9 on the main panel'. Suddenly the imagery disappears and I see the case files show up on the screen. 'It is all touch panel, Sam, show the General what you have.'

I spend what feels like hours running through the breadcrumbs with James and Gabby. The steps I took, how I followed the breadcrumbs to the café and why I thought this was Shadow, even why I thought Shadow was our guy. James wanted to know every detail; he would want clarity on every detail. It was overwhelming and exhausting, but my excitement of the chase was still evident. I wanted to go into detail on everything, to relive the feeling. The frustration, the excitement and the breakthroughs.

I did it though. I proved my worth. I grabbed the bull by the horns and swung it over my shoulder before just strolling through the office like it was nothing. I have made my mark, proved myself to the team. Maybe now they will respect me a little.

THE WARRANT

I AM SITTING IN AN SUV with an Australian Signals Directorate (ASD) strike team, assault rifles, pistols and Kevlar from head to toe. We are in a convoy of about six vehicles, all full of a similar level of weaponry. It's 5 pm on a Sunday. We have been watching the mark since I pinned down his offline identity and they don't want to wait any longer or he might get suspicious. So we have a warrant and are heading to storm the castle so to speak. I think he is going to get a nice surprise when all these men break down his door. I know I certainly would if it was me on that side of that door when they smash it down.

I will be waiting in the SUV until the site is secured and the castle has been successfully stormed. I am here to gather further evidence that can help our team connect Shadow to the crimes. Gabby and some others are here as well from our team in the other SUV's so it helps me relax a little. I think if I was on my own I would be very nervous about what is ready to unravel in the next few minutes.

We pull up just around the corner from Shadow's location and wait for the green light to proceed. It seems like hours before we get the go-ahead, but I believe it has only been fifteen minutes. The hairs on my arms are standing on end, my skin is almost electrified with excitement. The SUVs lurch into action, approaching the target at dramatic speed. Three take the back lane and the other three surge to a stop in the front of the property. The strike team all rush to their positions, they pause for must have been seconds till they were all in place, they entered the building and, in a few seconds, and some loud shouts had the property, the suspect and two other residents secured. After a few more minutes, one of them comes back and lets us know that we are now clear to enter the building.

I gather my gear from the SUV and head into the house. As I walk into the main area, I can see three suspects handcuffed sitting at the dining table. I see the mark, Loxley. He looks very calm and collected, unlike the others. They are being watched by two armed soldiers and are not going anywhere. As I get a little closer, he looks up at me and looks deep into my eyes. He has a brilliant blue colour to his eyes and is very good looking. It's a real shame he is a criminal.

I divert my eyes and focus on the job at hand. I need to find his computer equipment, his hidden data or anything that can help our case. Gabby takes the lead and gathers up phones, computers, and any storage devices. The warrant allows the collection and seizure of all electronic devices that could potentially hold data that would help to secure a conviction of the suspect. There is a lot of stuff and the cataloguing of it all is painful. We need to ensure a perfect log of events and chain of custody is kept or the case could be thrown out.

Shadow is silent though, too calm. I have a feeling he doesn't have anything here. He must have a setup away from home or he is certain we won't find anything on these devices. We might need to do some more digging. Maybe he knew we were coming. I guess we may never know.

Suddenly, I smell something burning. The suspect turns to the guard. 'Can someone please get my roast out of the oven before it turns to jerky? Maybe let us eat some of it why you are at it?' One of the soldiers grabs a cloth and pulls out his roast. It does look like it should have come out about an hour ago. The guard plonks it down on the sink and turns off the oven. 'I take it we won't be eating our dinner anytime soon then?' the guard just gives him a look and settles back into his job.

We gather and tag items for about another hour. The three guys are taken away during that time, back to an offsite interrogation facility most likely. When we are finished, one of the soldiers collects the locked storage and escorts it out to one of the SUVs for transport back to base. I think our work has only just begun, a lot of equipment to get through and report on. The next few days are not going to be as exciting as today was. The raid was a rush to be involved with. I can only imagine what it must be like to be one of the strike team, the first through the door. The chaos, the noise, the thrill of it all. Your whole body would be alive. Back to reality now for me and back behind the keyboard.

ZERO EVIDENCE

NOTHING, we have absolutely nothing. For two days, we have scoured every single device that was collected during the raid. Phones, laptops, desktops and so many storages drives, all empty of anything relevant. Now one thing I can say for sure, those guys who lived with Shadow really liked their porn. Now I have no issues with people enjoying their sexuality, doing what is pleasurable as long as it doesn't hurt anyone else, but wow, I have never seen that much porn ever. I have seen a lot in my adventures into the deep crevices of the deep web, beyond what many refer to as the dark web. Almost into nothing, it is like diving to the very depths of the deepest parts of the ocean. You can find beauty but you can also find things that will keep you from sleeping permanently if you don't have the stomach for it.

These guys though had something of almost everything, some stuff was just so weird that I have no idea what would even bring someone to ever want to do or see that kind of thing, but strangely everything is within the confines of the law. Nothing illegal, very bloody strange, but perfectly fine to have and view if that is what floats your boat. I need to get that stuff out of my head though. I need to sanitise my brain and just forget I ever saw any of that. I am never going to think of it again, ever.

Where was I? Right, no evidence of any kind relating to Shadow. It is almost like he didn't even live in the house. The only thing that was his was a mobile phone which had no history. All it had was a few pretty uneventful calls from utility providers or maintenance people for his house, which appeared to be rented all legitimately. Nothing was out of the ordinary, nothing at all. As far as the evidence and the rest of the world, Shadow is Jacob Thomas, but the history for Jacob only went back two years, before that it was like he didn't exist, which he probably didn't. Same as the Loxley surname that helped me track him down, all dead ends.

It is obvious that this was an identity constructed by Shadow to use as his daily cover, I don't even have any clues as to who he was before that, but I am certain even that identity would be just another cover. We have absolutely no way of tracing him back to a real identity if he even still has one somewhere.

I need to find something though, otherwise, James is going to lose it. He is already questioning whether my mark was real or if I have made a mistake. He and the rest of the team are doubting everything I found, thinking we have the wrong person. They are thinking we should let him go and get back to the drawing board. I don't want that to happen.

I know this is Shadow, he is the flesh and blood of the ghost they have been chasing for years now. I know it.

I make my way to the interrogation room viewing area and sit at the back of the room. I want to listen to the interrogation. It's the fourth time they have questioned Jacob and the answers never change. It's a rehearsed, perfected cover; he doesn't slip up once. He is truly gifted, that is for sure. A little arrogant, but gifted. I am told he has asked twice if he could get the number of 'the pretty brunette forensics girl', me, from his interrogators.

You are getting integrated for some serious crimes, threatened to be sent to a hole in the desert, left there to rot and he wants to set up a date with the pretty girl who came to investigate his crimes. To go through that weird-ass porn collection he and his friends had. I get a bit of a shiver down my spine just thinking of it. He indicates that the collection was his roommates and they were selling it to university students, that's how they were paying for their accommodations and constant parting. I guess that explains the size and variety of the collection.

This goes on and on for hours. They aren't getting anywhere with him at all. So I head back to the lab to have one more pass at the equipment, even though I know it is a waste of time. I need to do something though, all this sitting around is driving me crazy. A few more hours go by and I am at a wall, nothing. Nothing illegal except maybe some of the movies they have, some of them are more than likely downloaded illegally, but we don't care about any of that, that's not who we hunt, that's not what we are tasked to do. Piracy is someone else's concern. We are here for the worst of the worst, the ones no one else can catch.

I better go tell James and Gabby I have come up trumps, the big fat zero. This is not going to go well for me at all but what can I do. It is not like I can just pull the evidence out of thin air, although I wish I was some sort of magician and could pull the rabbit out of the hat, so to speak, but alas I am not…

BACK TO THE DRAWING BOARD

🗗

WHEN I FOUND the missing crumbs I needed to find Shadow a few weeks ago, or even two days ago when we were getting ready to raid his house, I did not think I would be getting strips torn off me by James. I was his star, the one who caught the uncatchable ghost, the only one on the team who had tried and actually gotten anywhere with it. I wasn't the only one who had tried though, several of them had tried over the years. I think that is why the dossier was so big. They could find whispers of what he had done, no tracers of a name, not even his hacker handle but I had done it, solo none the less.

Now I am an embarrassment, one that will cost us all, or at least me, the way this is playing out. James is not happy at all. He thinks I have completely messed this up, that this was a mistake and we have been harassing the wrong guy for two days.

The whole team has been analysing my work over the last few hours, trying to figure out where the mistake is, how we or should I say I have got this so wrong or if I am right and he is who I say he is. I need to figure out a way I can prove it or James said they will have to let him go with an apology. If they let Jacob, Shadow, whatever his name is, go we will never see him again.

Jacob will cease to exist; he will become someone new. This time though he will be more secure than he was before, more prepared. If he can dissolve and vanish I don't know if I will ever be able to find him again. I don't think that will matter though, as I won't likely get the chance to try. I will be out of a job. I don't know if that will stop me though, I will still hunt him for the rest of my life.

I don't think I would be able to stop the hunt, it's the same anytime I start a project, once I put my mind to the task it won't rest until its complete. Something in my brain that just won't let it go. Like a predator with the smell of blood in their nostrils, their animal instincts just take over. They do what they have been made to do. I am just like that hunter, once I flick that switch there is no going back.

'Let me talk to him, let me talk hacker to hacker. I can get him to slip up. He is arrogant and he will slip up.' James stares at me, arms folded over his chest.

'It is out of the question. You are not talking to him, I think you have done enough, don't you think? Don't make me regret my decision to bring you on board. Let this one go. You made a mistake, it happens. We all do it sometimes, even me. Let's go back to the drawing board, go back to your search find where you deviated and track down the real Shadow.'

I head back to my desk and do as James instructed. I review everything I have collected. I review the video footage,

I re-analyse the photo from the two girls, I even go back to the trail that led me to the café in the first place; it still all comes to the same result. Everything still points to him.

Think Sam, think. There has got to be something I can do.

I go back to the dark web, trying to find anything that I missed. There has to be another mistake, something. I know there has to be. It's time to rattle the cage and see what falls out. I find some more chatter about a raid and that a whale has been harpooned, do you think they are talking about us. I hone in on the chatter, but find nothing of value.

I could use this to my advantage. If they know we've got him, will they get a little more courageous and speak up? If the fear is gone or at least subsided and they feel a little more confident, their arrogance might kick in. It's a common problem in the hacker world, too many people with egos the size of houses. I think it's time Foresight should come out to play, show some thugs that Shadow is not the only one who should be feared in this place.

I do a call out for Shadow. I indicate he has done me wrong and I want retribution. It is risky. If I am wrong and he is still out there, he might come after me. I can handle it if he does but I don't think it's something I am going to have to worry about. If I am right, he won't be around to stop me and I might get one of the low hanging fruit who knows something to give me what I need to know. I am running out of time. I need to shake the cage and shake it hard, something needs to fall out. It has too. If I can't find something soon, we will have to let him go. So desperate measures it is; that's all I have got left. Here goes nothing, I make my move.

A few hours go past and nothing. Not a single peep from anyone at all. It has to be Shadow sitting in our interrogation room, otherwise he would be out to get me by now, but silence is all I am getting. I take down the post and do one last sweep of the marketplaces and forums.

Still, nothing that can help. I am out of road. Now, it is over. Shadow wins this round.

CATCH AND RELEASE

I'M SITTING HERE watching the interrogators have one last run at Shadow. We all know that it is a waste of time. Some are starting to think it's not even him to start with. That I have completely screwed this up and we have all been doing this for nothing. Just harassing some poor college kid, whose friends are just guilty of having too much porn.

I had some doubts at first myself, I admit, but he is Shadow. I have no doubts in my mind now at all. I have triple checked everything and it all leads to Jacob Loxley. A 19-year-old college student who doesn't really go to college, just seems to scrape through so he can still go to parties and hang out with idiots like his roommates.

The interrogators have been nice to him, tried to be his friends, tried to manipulate him into slipping up and giving something away. Now they are starting to threaten him.

'Listen here you little punk, we know you have been up to some really bad things. We know you are a hacker and we have proof you are involved in several high-profile incidents. Save us all some time and just confess to it so we can all just go home and you can get some food? I could potentially organise a nice roast meal to be brought to you in your cell since you missed out on your own?'

Jacob just looks at him and smiles 'You have the wrong guy. The porn isn't mine, that's my roommates. I don't have anything to do with any of that stuff.'

The interrogator sits down. 'We don't think you have any involvement with the unusually high volume of porn. That's not the issue here.'

Jacob doesn't seem surprised by that answer. 'So if you aren't trying to get me in trouble for all of that stuff, what do you want me for then? I don't know anything else. I can't be this hacker you keep mentioning, I can barely use the internet.' He pauses for a moment looking at the mirror wall that we are all watching through. 'I don't know who you think I am, but I swear I don't know who that is or anything about hacking. I think you have held me here for long enough. I want a lawyer and I want out of here unless you are going to charge me with something?'

The interrogators get up and leave the room. We won't be getting any sort of confession from this guy, even if he is the one we have been chasing. A few minutes go by and they re-enter the room and take a seat.

'Mr Loxley, we would like to apologise for the extended delay in your release. We have had strong reasons to think you are connected to these crimes and we still believe you are not as innocent as you make out you are. Even if you are not the hacker we are after, your hands are not clean here.'

He looks at him for a moment and then continues, 'we will be arranging for your release today. It may take another hour or so to get the paperwork finalised and then you will be taken back to your home by our team. You need to understand something very clearly now, we will be watching you very closely Mr Loxley. We will be making sure that you are as you say. Don't leave town. If you try to leave town, we will arrest you and hold you as a flight risk until you have been completely cleared by our investigators. Do you understand?'

Jacob, Shadow, nods.

Another hour passes and I see them put a bag over his head and escort him out of our complex, he is being released and taken back home. I have failed he is getting away with this.

I take some nice, calm, deep breaths. I feel a hand on my shoulder. It's Gabby.

'Don't let this get you down. We had to let him go. We don't have enough to hold him, it's all circumstantial and doesn't directly pin him to any crime. That doesn't mean you have to give up if you still believe it is him. Keep watch. If it is him, he knows now we are on to him, he will make a move. You just need to be ready to spot it.' Gabby is right, this isn't over.

This case is still mine for the moment. James hasn't taken me off it yet, although I think my rope is shortening by the minute. I need to be patient, wait for his next move, wait for his next mistake so I can pounce.

I will be watching, Shadow. It's your move.

CALM BEFORE THE STORM

⧉

I TOOK A FEW DAYS OFF, trying to unwind and forget about the whole mess. It has been almost two weeks now since Shadow was released from custody. The team has been watching him 24/7. He is being physically surveilled with a couple of teams on him at all times, his home and phone are bugged and everything he does online is analysed with a fine-tooth comb to ensure he isn't communicating in some sort of code or initialising some sort of attack.

Nothing though, absolutely nothing. If this guy is for real, he has a boring life. He doesn't go anywhere, he doesn't hang out with many people. He will attend a couple of weekend parties, but from what I have seen, he doesn't fit in, he is an outsider of sorts. Generally liked, but he seems to keep his distance. It sounds a little familiar. There is a lot of similarities between Shadow and myself. It scares me a little that I could have gone down the same path if James hadn't approached me, steered me down the better path. Who knows how this all could have turned out. I might have been the one in that interrogation room, not for recruitment, but for crimes I had committed.

I think I have been watching this guy too long. He is starting to get into my head. I have taken the mustang out for a drive, a nice windy road with deep twists and turns. Lots of places for speed and some for precision. I just love it, it gets me out of my head. I concentrate and push the car to the edge of its limits. It clears all of my thoughts, it's the only thing that does.

I have been pushing the car hard today. It's taking it in its stride though. Each turn I push it hard, hearing the grumble of the engine, the vibrations of its power shuddering through the entire car. My heart is pumping hard in my chest and I feel exhilarated. If I push it any harder, I will either lose my licence or they will be scraping me out of this car at the bottom of a cliff, but I keep pushing, keep asking more and more of the car. I am creeping towards its limit; I can feel it but I don't want to stop. Brrrrp Brrrrp Burp, my phone vibrates on the hard plastic of the centre console. I snap back to reality; I am going to be late.

I head back home, it's Friday and movie night with Dad. I will enjoy the distraction and companionship if I am honest. These long hours have taken it out of me and I know I have started to become a little obsessed. There are little black smudges under my eyes, it's time to take a breath and get a new perspective.

I wonder what Shadow is doing. What's his plan? He must have one. Is he just going to ride this whole thing out and just weather the storm? Does he think it will work? Does he have the patience and resolve to stick it out and do absolutely nothing? Could I do it if it was me in his place? I think I could.

I would have pretended that I was just Sam, forgot Foresight for a while, even though it is a part of me, it could be left dormant and I could hide that side of me I know I could. It would eventually get the better of me though and I would get sloppy, he will do the same. Even if I am given another assignment, I will keep watch. I will get him if I am patient.

I turn the corner near my home and see Dad's truck in the driveway. A smile comes across my face, I am happy to see him. Time to forget about Shadow for today and get back to my life for tonight, at least.

THIN AIR

I GET UP EARLY. I have enjoyed my few days off and feel like they have helped. I am clear minded again and ready to get back to work, to hunt down my prey. I am a hacker. I am Foresight, I can do this. I check my outfit in the mirror and head downstairs, I am having a quick breakfast with Dad today. He is waiting for me as I come downstairs, he has what looks to be an omelette for each of us. I sit down and start to eat. We casually chat about everything, except my work, he knows I can't discuss that. He has gotten used to that and doesn't ask anymore, which is easier, so I don't have to lie or just refuse to tell him anything.

I get about halfway through and then my phone starts to go crazy. Gabby is calling me at 7 am, that's weird. I will call her back when I finish breakfast. My phone jumps to life again. It's another member of our team now. I consider picking it up when I am startled by a knock at the door, who in the hell would that be at this time of day? What could have happened that would warrant all of this?

Dad gets up and heads to the door.

A few seconds later he sings out, 'Sam it's for you, you're needed at work, urgently'. I pick up my bag and leave my half-eaten breakfast on the breakfast bar.

'I have to go, I am sorry to leave in the middle of our breakfast.' He looks at me and starts to shake his head.

'Don't worry about it Sam, if they are going to all of this trouble to get your attention it must be important. Be safe Kiddo.' I walk through the door. The driver has already returned to the SUV and is waiting for me, the door open. He doesn't say anything to me just closes the door after I climb in.

He quickly gets back in the SUV and he takes off with similar aggression to when the raid was executed.

'What is going on? What has happened?' he looks at me in the mirror for a split second.

'Sorry Sam, that's a little above my pay grade, I don't know anything except I need to get you to the office as fast as I can.'

The driver takes his assignment seriously. I hope we can't get a speeding ticket in this vehicle, as I am certain he has run a few red lights and flew past a few stationary cameras. We enter through the usual way and Gabby is waiting for me at the doors of the elevator.

'Sam you need to come with me. You were right about Jacob, he is Shadow.' My interest level has peaked.

'What has happened, how do you know I am right? Did he make a move?' She turns to me with an almost panicked look on her face.

'He has vanished, in thin air. Almost like he never existed. He slipped his tail sometime during the night. They searched.

He couldn't be found anywhere. Everyone is trying to find him. James wants you on this, he thinks you are the only one who wasn't fooled. You found him in the first instance, you can do it again.'

Wow, this is not good. We may never find him if he gets away. I knew I didn't mess this up. As I enter the lab, everyone is chaotic. People are rushing around in almost a complete frenzy. James is, however, standing next to my desk as I approach. Waiting for me, it would seem.

'Morning Sam, it would seem as though you have arrived at a mess for you to clean up for me. Has Gabby filled you in?'

I nod, glancing at the older woman, still standing by my side. 'A little'.

He gestures for me to follow him as he walks, 'Come with me please, I would like to discuss something with you in private If I may?' I do as directed and walk with him back to the elevator and step in when he does. Gabby watches us leave, a pinched expression on her face. He doesn't say anything more until the elevator doors are closed. 'Sam, we have a real mess now to clean up and it is one that we could have avoided if we had all just listened to you. I give you my word, after all this is over, I will not question your resolve or motives again. I will take you on your word when you tell me something, even if it's hard to accept.' The elevator stops and we step out into his office, we have the full-body scan and the doors open. We walk in and he continues 'I need you to fix this for me, I don't care how, do what you do best, use those amazing skills we both know you have. I know you are holding back, you don't need to.

You have my authority to do what is needed. Take this bastard down, get him back in custody so I can put him in a hole somewhere.'

'Consider it done General. But can I clarify, *whatever* it takes?'.

He smiles at me now. 'Exactly what that sounds like Sam. Break whatever laws you have to. Hack any systems you need, do whatever it takes but do it fast before this mess of ours gets run up the food chain by one of the ambitious analysts out there who would love my job. Is that clear?'

I nod. 'Get it done, and fast. I gotcha...'

THE EXPLOSION

I START TO HEAD BACK upstairs to get to work on finding Shadow when the phone rings.

'Wait, Sam this could be something relevant for you.' I pause. James just listens, whatever they are saying seems to interest him. 'I want Sam on this, get a team out there and take her with you. Anything she needs, she gets. Understood?' I don't know what they said on the other side but whatever it is, it looks like I am going somewhere.

James hangs up the phone. 'There has been an explosion, they have found an underground bunker in the forest a few miles outside of town. It was full of computer equipment by the looks of the debris that is scattered all over the place. I want you out there, find something you can use. Remember what I said Sam, whatever it takes but get it done fast. Gabby will meet you upstairs. This is your case, so direct the team as you need them.' I nod and turn, leaving the room.

I get upstairs and join the team. We gather up our go bags and head out. It doesn't take long before we arrive. The hole in the ground from the explosion is huge, if this was Shadow's handy work, he didn't want to leave anything behind for us to use against him. As we near the scene, the police stop us. Gabby says something to them and the officer radios something to his command. A few moments later, he waves us through no further questions asked.

Shards of electronic equipment are everywhere, nothing is in one piece. We all climb out of the SUV and I walk up closer to the crater in front of us. I have never seen anything like this before. It's what I imagine a war zone looks like. Everything is scorched, glass and twisted metal are laying everywhere. This is not going to be easy.

Suddenly, I realise the rest of the team are looking at me, starring actually. Oh right, I am in charge here. I consider what needs to be done for a few moments and look over the scene. 'Find something we can use, there has to be some evidence in there that has survived. Catalog it all and let's get what we can use back in the lab.' They nod and disperse, just getting to work. It must piss them off a little that I am in charge and a month ago I was basically their overpaid intern, the coffee girl.

How things have changed. They are not complaining though. they are doing what they need to. The order has come down from the General, after all. No one will question this, especially in the mood he is in today and the mess that we need to get under control. I am in charge and that's the end of it, for now at least.

I guess they feel if this all goes south, further than it has already, I will be the fall girl. They are probably right, this could be the end for me if I can't fix this mess, it could be the end for the General too. I don't want that to happen. He has stuck his neck out for me. It is my job to get him off the chopping block now.

The next few hours go past with a blur. We are digging through this mess, trying to put the jigsaw puzzle back together. We have nothing though, nothing at all. The explosion was a success. We will not be getting anything off any of the junk we pull out of this crater we have here. Shadow made sure of that.

We stick at it for another five or six hours before we have tagged and bagged anything of potential. We load it all up into the secure evidence storage and take it back into the office. When we get there, I tell the team to work on everything we have, find something in the pile of rubbish that we can get data off. Before I finish, my phone rings, it's the General.

'I want an update. What do you have?'

I take a breath before responding. 'We don't have anything; everything is too damaged. I don't think we will get anything of use from anything we have collected, I will need to find another way to find him.'

There is silence on the other end for a few moments, long enough for me to start to think he might have hung up on me.

'Do what it takes, Sam. I don't know how long I can hold off this heat. At least find me some concrete evidence he is who you said he was that might be enough to buy us some time for you to hunt. Go get your prey, Sam.' Then the phone goes dead. Okay, so he really did hang up on me this time. I need to get to work now find something we can use. It's time for Foresight to find him, not Sam.

This is going to be tough. I need to focus. I can do this. I know I can.

BREADCRUMBS

I'VE BEEN AT THIS for hours, I know I have, but it seems to have gone past in the blink of an eye. I have been in an almost trance just hunting, searching and nudging for information. I have gained access to a few different law enforcement agency systems. I didn't ask permission, but I am sure they will understand. James did say I was to do whatever it takes, so that's what I am doing.

I've found a few leads I didn't have before so it's been worth the effort to glean the additional information. It would have taken me weeks or at least hours to find it on my own. I have a feeling that he is heading north, just seems logical due to the bunker being south of his home. He would have known it was going to explode, or he set it off in person at the site so he would want to go the opposite direction. At least that's what I would do.

Maybe he will head south just because he thinks we will all assume he will head north as well. Oh, I have no idea, I just need to stop overthinking this and find something concrete to go on.

My facial recognition software springs to life. I have a hit. It's only the fourth time this has happened already, so I am not getting my hopes up just yet, but maybe this time it will be something useful. They have all been partial matches with poor angles or something blocking the view, but nothing I could say was a real match or even a potential. This one isn't much better, but it does have a side view of the face, it's from a traffic camera heading through the sunshine coast, I clear up the footage, re-process it. I think this could be him, it looks like a good match. He is heading north. I knew it.

He is driving some sort of SUV, a dark colour. I think it is a cayenne. He must be heading somewhere in a hurry to want one of those. It's not the most inconspicuous vehicle though. I am guessing he was more concerned about having a quick getaway if he needed it. Those Porsche Cayennes are not for the faint-hearted, that's for sure. I will check if there is one that has been reported stolen recently. I jump over to the Queensland police service systems to see what I can dig up; nothing has been reported in Queensland, a couple in Victoria, but nothing that could be our suspect. I have to track that car, somehow, I need to know where it is going.

I might be able to find it if I break into the Porsche vehicle tracking system or PVTS for short. I should be able to correlate the timestamps from when Shadow was first seen and then narrow down the potential vehicles that he could be driving, as I would assume he is. I set aim at their systems. This shouldn't take me too long.

I scan their perimeter defences and there's a little push back from the protections. Normally, I would step back and just keep lightly testing the surface, find a soft spot in the armour before poking and prodding, squeezing my way silently through the cracks that were forming, but I don't have days or even hours to do this gently. I need access and I need it now. I hope James meant it when he said to do whatever is needed.

I take a deep breath, close my eyes for a few moments, another deep breath.

Now...

I get to work, throwing everything I have at the defences. I twist when they attack, I bend and turn, manoeuvring at rapid speed. I start to let my instincts lead me deeper into the depths of the system. It is getting noisy, they know I am here, they are trying to hold me back but bit by bit I am pushing deeper and deeper. I can feel them buckling under the pressure. Now is my time to make my move.

I throw my DDoS attack platform at their sales systems, everything I have. I need to make some noise. I need them to be focused on fighting me off so they can't notice my sleight of hand or the game will be up and I'll have to find a new way to get what I want.

It's time. Like a whisper in the night, no trace, no sound. I manipulate the firewall and execute my takeover sequence. I have access. I have full control of the perimeter network. Easy now Sam, easy now, do this right. We only have one shot at this. I manoeuvre to the server cluster, softly looking for my way to take control but make it quiet, I find it. I execute my exploit kit, taking advantage of an unpatched vulnerability, it works, I have control. I let them battle against my zombie swarm. It is almost completely crippling them, I am impressed, they are putting up a really good fight.

They make their move now, starting by dropping all my malicious packets at the perimeter, locking them down, taking unnecessary systems offline. They are smart, reducing the attack surface, very clever indeed, well maybe if I wasn't already inside watching them on the sidelines with a metaphorical bucket of popcorn. This is quite fun, I needed a good digital dual. Something to help me relax a little and just enjoy my craft for a few minutes. It is probably time I let them win though, I send my back down command sequence to the swarm and they slowly die down, making it look as though they have been defeated.

A few minutes go by, everything stops, not a move. I am in but the rest of my attacks are stopped. I lay silent, play dead. I am counting on them thinking they have won. I want them to think they have fought off the boogie man. They are very wrong. I smile. I am the the scary thing hiding in the dark to scare poor naughty children at night or in this instance the IT and security teams at Porsche. I was starting to make them have a bad night but believing they beat me back should give them an ego boost at least until they figure out it was all just a show for their sake, a distraction from the truth. They just let me through the front door and invited me to dinner without even knowing they had done it. I wonder how long it will take them to catch on if they even do at all.

I don't think I should be enjoying this so much, but this is me, this is Foresight in my true sense. Does this make me more like Shadow than I want to admit? After all, this is what he does. He takes down bad people who have done really bad things, yeah, he takes their money, but he gives most of it to charities. Yes, some still lines his pockets but I assume keeping up his facade wouldn't be cheap and nothing in that bunker of his would have been either. Am I really justifying his actions in my head? I need to shake this off, I have a job to do.

Enough playtime. It's time to find Shadow.

After a quick review of the cars around Shadow's last known area, there are only three that could be him. One belongs to a lawyer and it is heading the wrong way, it isn't our guy. Another car's last known location was at a storage facility and it hasn't moved in weeks. The last looks like it's owned by a retired couple that uses it for shopping by the looks of the recent movements. Wow, that would be a quick shopping car.

Regular trips back and forth to the shops but not much else. It probably never goes over 80, nope, guess again. I just looked over the information. The car has recently spiked at over 140 on multiple occasions, I am impressed this old couple can drive if it is them driving it.

The obvious choice would have been the storage facility vehicle, but something about the retiree's car seems off, apart from the speed for one that the old couple is capable of, it just feels strange. I check if it is active. It has been offline for nearly two days. It doesn't mean anything though; they just might not be big drivers and it could be just sitting at home in their garage.

To be safe, I check out the vehicle more closely. I see if I can trigger a remote GPS reactivation, see if the systems will allow remote override of the user commands. It's a feature many car manufacturers add in these days to help track down stolen cars. Not one that is always mentioned to budding buyers though, many wouldn't like the fact that it can be reactivated remotely even after you manually switch it off. People might find out about their extramarital activities, or who they like to hang out with in their spare time. It never surprises me to find backdoors or hidden features like these though. I am honestly more surprised when they don't exist.

The car's computer systems are struggling with the request. I don't think it likes me forcing it to bend to my will but in the end, it does what I want and I ping the car's location. It responds with current location and speed. We have some of those new cameras in that area, the ones that are designed to catch mobile phone users on their phones while driving. It's great for that but it's also good for my facial recognition platform. I built this code years ago to help me target the thugs and crime gangs.

It was the easiest way to find all the assets and figure out the best way to hurt them. It always helps if you have all the information to a puzzle. It helped me inflict some pain at the time and I am certain that they had no idea how I knew what I did. How I could target them in ways that crippled their operations, I am certain they probably thought I was an insider, a mole in their house. Tearing them apart from within. If they knew I was a teen hacker with a cause, they would be surprised, maybe mortified, that I inflicted so much chaos. Maybe the fact I was a girl would have been the icing on the cake.

This is the perfect tool for this job, fast, efficient and that's what I need right now. It only takes me a few minutes to find him. It is time to move in slowly and take him down. No catch and release this time around. I call in the strike team, watching his every move while they get into positions.

It takes less than 15 minutes to have them in place. We must have teams we can call on all over the country or they flew them in by helicopter or something crazy like that. None of that matters though. They are ready. That's all I need to know. Okay, let's do this. I give them a green light. They move in closer, getting ready to pounce on the target. He has stopped in a back street; the team now has him surrounded. They move in quickly and are on top of the target in seconds.

Nothing from the team, it's silence. What the hell is going on? Somebody give me an update already. I look at all the body cam feeds, the car door is open, but he is nowhere to be seen. Arrrgh, we have lost him again, this can't be happening.

'Spread out, search the area. He's there somewhere.' James won't be happy if we let him slip through our fingers when we are so close.

HUNTER BECOMES THE HUNTED

⊡

I WALK THROUGH the door, I see Dad watching me from the kitchen as I enter.

'You look tired. I think you might be working too hard. You need to have something to eat and then get yourself some sleep. If you keep this up, you'll burn out and be no good to anyone. What you do is important but you need to remember you are important too. Sit down I will fix you something before I go to work'. I don't argue, he's right I haven't been looking after myself. I have let the hunt for Shadow take over everything else, sleep, food, none of it mattered as much as catching him.

I take a seat and watch him work. After a few moments I can smell the aroma drifting over, I wasn't hungry before but that smell, it's amazing. I guess I really was hungry and I just needed Dad's cooking to remind me. He puts down some food in front of me, bacon and eggs. Just what I need, he makes me a coffee as well. I take a bite of bacon, its crunchy, salty and just amazing. I can feel my stomach grumble.

I am lucky to have him, he is a good father. I'll need to tell him that sometime, I don't have the energy right now for that though.

He kisses me on the forehead. 'Get some rest, okay? I am heading to work.' His keys jingle as he collects them from the hook by the door. 'We still on for movie night tonight?'

'Of course, I wouldn't miss it,' I say, stifling a yawn with the back of my hand. He smiles, he enjoys our movie nights even more now that I am out so often. His busy, secret cyber spy is an in-demand girl. No one else knows what I do and it must kill him that he can't shout it out from the roof that his little girl is beating back the cyber threats of our world. I think he is proud of what I am doing, maybe a bit worried I don't look after myself but proud none the less.

He walks out the door and I hear him drive away. I quickly finish my meal, I'm unsure if it counts as my breakfast, or dinner, but it's good either way, then head up to bed. Dad is right, I need to get some sleep. A fresh mind will do me wonders. I must have fallen asleep almost as soon as my head hit the pillow as the first thing I hear is the front door close, it can't be afternoon already. I look over at the clock on my bedside table, wow it is 6 pm, Dad is late. I feel my tummy growl. I can smell the Chinese from here. Time to get up.

That night, we watch a couple of movies and pig out on our usual movie snacks. You can never go wrong with salty butter popcorn and snakes to back it up. It was a great night. Dad heads to bed around 11 pm but thanks to my earlier nap, I am not tired so decide to do some work. At my desk,

I think back on simpler days when it was just me against the underworld. It feels like forever since I was at school, it has been months since I was pretending to be a normal girl while living a double life as Foresight. I guess I am still pretending as far as the rest of the world goes, but now Foresight is not a lone hacker with a cause. I am part of an army. It fills me with pride thinking that I am part of something bigger, but I do still miss those simpler days.

I fire up my laptop and a message pops up from an anonymous user: *I hear you are looking for me.* Could this be Shadow? Holy crap, what should I do? I think it over for a moment, deciding I should play along, It could help me find him.

Who are you? I hit send.

A reply only takes a few moments. *I am Shadow. You already know that though, don't you Foresight?* Okay, he knows my hacker self, what else does he know?

Yes, I do. I send and get an almost instant response like he had already written his response but was just waiting for me to respond first.

So, what set your sights on me? Whose toes did I step on to ruffle your feathers? Or do you just want to prove you are the best in the schoolyard? Ugh. *You have done some cool things, I'm impressed, a perfect girl.* He's trying to push my buttons. He doesn't seem scared of me, but it seems as though he might respect me. He knows I am a girl, or at least suspects I am. It's not something I have ever mentioned anywhere as Foresight.

Maybe he knows who I am. Oh crap, I hope not. That's all I need, this bloody hacker with a revenge trip coming to my home. *I will take that as a compliment,* I reply. I pause for a few more moments trying to consider how I approach this.

You take what isn't yours, I don't like that. You might target scum bags but you do it for profit not for good. I watch the screen, he has gone quiet, maybe I took that too far. Maybe I have pissed him off.

A few minutes go by before I get his response, it was starting to drive me crazy waiting.

It's true, I make money from the scum of the earth. It is expensive staying invisible and the money I take was never really theirs in the first instance. We don't all work for Government agencies do we, Sam? Crap, he knows who I am. *We don't all have unlimited resources and an army of helpers. Some of us have to make the best of what we have.*

Well, I guess there is no need for games anymore.

Why don't you just turn yourself in and save me the headache of finding you? Trust me on this: I will find you.

I was hoping you would say that. I love games, none before you have tested me as much. This is going to be fun, may the best hacker win...

That's the last message I get. I guess he wants to play, set his skills against my own, I wonder what that means, what is he going to do next. I hope this doesn't get too messy, but it does mean I will have more opportunities to track him.

The remainder of the night is uneventful. I do a bit of searching and then decided to get a good night's sleep. If it's game on, I need to be on my best footing. It doesn't start that way the next day though, I am startled awake by loud music. I think it is 'Thunderstruck' belting from the lounge room at full volume. What the hell? I meet Dad at the top of the stairs. We both look at each other with a bit of a dazed look.

'I thought that must have been you down there. What the hell is going on? Stay up here for a minute while I check it out.' He gets about halfway down the stairs before I start to follow. He notices but doesn't argue.

We walk around the corner and see the smart speaker blaring at full volume. The time says 5 am and I see the playlist name: *Shadow*. Oh great, this is part of his game, I click on the screen swiping down the volume instantly, I click on the playlist and see that he has added in a lot of high energy, loud songs and has put the description as: *This should get you pumped and ready for battle*. Dad is searching the house for anyone who could be hiding but I know he won't find anyone.

'It's all clear, no one is here Sam. It must be just a technology spasm that caused that thing to go nuts on us at 5 am.' I nod and switch the speaker off at the wall. 'Do you want a coffee, since we are up now?'

'Sure. Sounds good Dad.'

I look back over at the speaker. Its game on Shadow, game on indeed.

It gets me thinking though, I wonder if Shadow is going to escalate this, will it get out of hand or is he just going to keep doing annouying pranks. I don't have to wait long to find out. It's only a few more minutes when the doorbell rings. Who in the hell would be at our door at 5 in the morning? Dad scowls and sets his mug down on the counter with a bang, clearly irritated. This could be interesting for whoever is on the other side of that door. I make my way to see who it is behind him. As he opens the door, I see an Uber eats delivery guy.

'What do you want? It's 5 am and we haven't ordered anything...' he seems thrown back by Dad's reaction and looks a little scared. I get it. Dad is a big guy and he looks pissed at the moment.

'Ummm I am very—ummm—Sorry sir. I have a breakfast delivery for two from a Mr Shadow for Sam and John. Is that you?' Dad looks puzzled 'Who the hell is Mr Shadow?' the driver looks more nervous now.

'I am sorry Sir, I don't know who Mr Shadow is. I just pick up the orders and deliver them.' He swallows loudly, the poor guy is packing it. 'It is a good delivery sir, it's two full English breakfasts. If you don't want them I can mark the order as fulfilled and eat these myself?' Dad almost looks disgusted with that idea and takes them out of his hands. 'That's fine we will take them.'

He mumbles, 'have a nice day sir.' Dad seems to be cooling off.

'You too buddy. Sorry for the temper, it's nothing personal. Just not good with unwanted 5 am wake ups.' I see the delivery guy click something on his phone he must be marking the delivery complete. A few seconds later I hear a notification on my phone upstairs, I turn and go upstairs to grab my phone. It's a notification from Uber eats, I paid for this bloody order.

Grrrrrr... Deep breath Sam, deep breath. Well, I paid for it, I might as well go eat it. On the way down the stairs, I change my passwords on the Uber app and set up multifactor authentication. I should already know better. It is what I do and I don't have it myself. I login and change my account connected to the smart speaker. I don't feel like another wake up like that.

I eat breakfast with Dad. The Uber Eats guy was right, this is really good stuff. I will have to remember this place when I want to order some breakfast myself. Thanks, Shadow, this one was not bad.

Ding dong...

The doorbell. Here we go again, Dad's face turns stony again. 'I'll get it Dad,' I say and I make my way to the door. I look through the peep hole and see it's another delivery of some sort. I reach down and open the door.

'Good morning Miss, I have a delivery for you. Where would you like it?' I look at him for a moment.

'What is it?' he looks puzzled.

'Are you not expecting a delivery?' I shake my head. He looks at his delivery slip.

'This is the right house; I have some bulk grocery supplies. I will bring them in.' I just nod, not much I can do about it now.

I watch him pull a pallet full of toilet paper out of the truck, nope, it's two pallets. What in the hell am I going to do with two pallets of toilet paper? He unloads them all in handfuls into our house before heading back to the truck. What now? It's bad enough I am going to have to try and return 150 max size packets of toilet paper. Now what. I look back and it's a massive bunch of flowers. Flowers? What is Shadow getting at? I see a card attached as the driver hands them over. He turns back and returns with two more boxes and sits them on the floor. 'That's all. Have a great day Miss.' He closes the door and leaves.

I wonder if the driver thinks this delivery is weird, or if he doesn't care. Dad stands in the living room, surrounded by toilet paper and flowers.

'What is going on Sam?'

I shake my head. 'I don't know exactly. 'Dad opens the boxes, one full of condoms, all different sizes. He raises an eyebrow at me.

'Well at least with all of this we can both be safe for the next 10 years.' He really doesn't look impressed at all, I wonder what he thinks is going on here. I wonder if he thinks its Michael sending me the big box of condoms. He was a little uncomfortable with us kissing, so I am certain this is going to really push him outside of his comfort zone.

He shakes his head with a bit of a smile on his face, he seems to be going with this, whatever the situation is. 'The toilet paper though, what in the hell can anyone do with that much toilet paper.' He shakes his head and turns back to the kitchen and his coffee.

I take the card from the flowers and open it up.

'I never got your number Sam. Now I do. I hope you like the flowers, I thought it is rude to not give flowers on a first date. This is kinda like a hacker's version of a first date, so here you are.' I smile, cheeky bastard. Flowers was a nice touch, not sure it goes with the box of condoms though. 'Hope you are enjoying our game so far, it's your move.'

I better do a security check, see what he is in already. As I work through everything, he has found his way into a few of my different accounts. I suddenly get a thought. Could he have gotten into my bank account? I better check. I login and look. Everything seems normal than I see it in the description of a $1 funds transfer: *Just so you know although I could, I don't take what isn't mine.*

I quickly change my details but then realise I already have admin control of this bank systems myself so it's likely Shadow does as well.

You want to play Shadow, let's play. I log into the bank servers and locate the IP for the machine that processed that $1 transaction. It was a Brisbane northside location. He is in Redcliffe. I try and narrow it down. I scan with my tools. He has to show up somewhere. How about I flush him out? I could shut down the power grid. That will stop him or at least slow him down. Is that crossing a line though, is that taking this too far?

Doing this will cut power to thousands of homes, is it justified to get a one up on a hacker? Screw it, whatever it takes, that's what the General said. I login to the grid. I send through my command. Power starts shutting down, everything is out. I start to see reports of widespread power outage across media with no one knowing what had happened. The chat pings to life: *Nice work Sam. I am looking forward to meeting you face to face again sometime soon.* I go to write back but stop as another message comes through: *Did you like your flowers?* He really is a smart aleck, this one.

'Yes thank you, but it turns out that I probably paid for them. So I should be thanking myself.'

A few moments later he comes back: *No actually I paid for that delivery, the flowers were all me. The toilet paper though that's all you* ☺

He paid for the order, at least in part. I can track him now, credit card, details something... *No point checking the transaction info Sam, it is not mine and it won't lead you back to me.* Bugger. It's my turn now, I track the phone number that the internet IP came through, I shut it down. Messages stop.

A few minutes later he is back: *Nice move Sam, you should probably turn the power back on though. I am moving on now anyway.* I turn the search scanning up to full power, I will find him. I see that the power outage is helping him stay in the shadows, so I switch it all back on and slowly I see the lights come back on. Then I see him, a wave at the camera then disappears into shadows. That was the last of the silly business. After that, it's all quiet. I wonder what his next move is.

Most of the rest of my Saturday continued on this path. I would make a move; he would make a move. There were no more deliveries, at least that was something. Neither of us could get the upper hand; it was tit for tat and I didn't see a clear path to win. I was enjoying this game, not that I would admit it to anyone or myself really but I was. Shadow was truly challenging me like no one else ever could. He is as close a match in skill as I had ever seen and it excited me to face off with him. To fight for dominance in this hidden world.

It was a surprise to me; one I had not anticipated.

NOT HOW I SAW THAT GOING

IT'S A NICE SUNDAY MORNING, and everything on the Shadow front has been quiet. He has been behaving himself mostly, still sending me messages now and then but no more strange deliveries. Seems like he just wants to talk shop and maybe it sounds like he likes me. I need to stay focused. I need to remember he is my target and I can't fall for this act.

It's time to take the beast for a drive, it will help me clear my mind. Nothing works better than a bit of petrol fumes and speed to make you feel better. I grab my keys and let Dad know I am heading out for a drive. He doesn't say anything, he does the same thing with the mustang most weekends as well to clear his thoughts, I think he might like my car more than I do. I back out of the driveway and launch down the road. I can feel my tension draining away already and I am only just getting started.

I have been driving for about half an hour when I spot a dark car that seems to be following me. Could it be Shadow? Could he be about to make a move in the real world? They accelerate closer behind me, it's a black BMW. I react without any real thought, accelerating aggressively. I surge forward but I don't lose them. They are sticking with me, struggling, but they are hanging on. Let's see what you have got Shadow. I push the mustang harder; I can hear the growl of the engine, I feel the hairs on my entire body stand up on end. This is exhilarating. We race through back roads heading out of the city to the south, down towards the gold coast at an insane speed. This is crazy, I should back off, but I am committed now.

It's a game of cat and mouse. I pull away and they gain some distance. Back and forth. I can't keep this up forever though. I need a plan to get out of this. Going home is not an option. I can't take him back to the house not near Dad. Think Sam, Think. How can I deal with this? Suddenly a car hits me from the side, it jams me hard into the cement barrier and my car launches up in the air and swings around, mounting a curb. The airbag has gone off; the car is screwed. Blood is coming from above my left eye, a lot of blood. Shit, I think my arm is dislocated. I brace myself and shove it back into place. I hear a pop, a sickening sound that makes me shudder in my core. That definitely looks easier when you see it in movies. My eyes go fuzzy, I'm going to pass out. Not now, not now, but it's too late.

It is dark, I have pain everywhere. That crash messed me up bad. I go to move my arms, hang on they are secured to a chair, my feet too. What the hell is happening here? Shadow has got me, crap. I need to figure out how to get out of this duct tape holding me in place. I struggle and squirm, but it's no good. I am stuck in this chair. I try to focus. I can see something shiny over the other side of the room I am in, it's knives, torture tools. This isn't what I would expect from Shadow. He is a hacker; I didn't peg him as a serial killer or torturer. Something isn't right about this situation.

Focus Sam, what is happening here? Suddenly I see them, someone is standing in the back corner of the room in the shadows. They step forward so I can see them. They hold my gaze for a moment.

'You took on the wrong crew, young lady. You almost took out our whole operation when you burnt down our data centre. It cost us billions, that's right billions. You are going to wish you died in that car crash by the time we are done with you. We are going to torture you, then we are going to rape you, and then we will start again and then again until you either die or we get bored with you. Then we will finally kill you.' He looks like he is enjoying this, he has a creepy kind of smile. I need to try and stay calm. I can feel my heart racing, my throat is dry and I am on the verge of vomiting. I can't lose control. Focus Sam.

My team and General James will come looking for me. I hope they will anyway and I hope it's not too late, this isn't how I pictured losing my virginity. Not in a million years.

I see a flicker of light. Suddenly, I see a camera move in the top corner of the room above the entrance. Someone is watching this. Who? The boss, whoever that it is I assume. It moves back and forth between myself and my torturer before settling on me. I guess the show is about to start. Lucky me...

The man looks over his tools, he has quite a collection. The usual pliers, needles, knives and hammers. All sorts of fun tools you can use to inflict pain on your victims. The worst part is that I am that victim. I don't know if I can handle this. I continue to look over them until he settles on a scalpel. He picks it up and turns back towards me. Get ready, this is not going to be pretty. I take a deep breath and close my eyes. Don't scream, really try not to scream Sam, don't make this fun for him. A single tear runs down my cheek, I am starting to lose my control, come on Sam, you can do it.

The first cut shocks my system, it is long but shallow. The pain is horrendous. I assume he wants to keep me alive, to make this last a long time. He does a second and a third all slowly to inflict as much pain on me as he can. I don't scream though. I fight it back. I will not give him the satisfaction. I can do this, hold it together. I watch as he positions the blade for another cut.

A massive explosion shakes the room, and he stops. Gunfire rings in the distance. What is happening? It's getting closer and closer. Suddenly the door is kicked in by a hooded soldier in complete black head to toe, several of them fill the room. One of them fires, shooting the torturer in the head. Some of his blood splatters on my face and he hits the ground near my feet, dead. I look up and one of the soldiers pulls out a knife and cuts the restraints from my arms and legs. Another secures his primary weapon and helps me to my feet.

'Can you walk?' he asks, and I nod.

'I can walk but I might need some help.' He nods and props me up on his shoulder before pulling out a pistol.

He barks a command, 'let's move'. It goes quickly, guns firing, people coming from everywhere, the soldiers killing them instantly. So many of them I don't even know how many. The walls everywhere are splattered with blood, parts of the building are missing. This is what a real war zone looks like, I don't need to imagine anymore. This is it.

We reach a van, and they pull me in before screaming away at speed. I look at the team around me, some of them have minor wounds, nothing major though by the looks, none of them takes off the balaclavas. These must be the General's men, he sent them to rescue me, didn't he? But they don't look familiar at all. Maybe it's the shock, but I guess it doesn't matter who they are, just that they came for me.

We drive for what seems like 30 minutes, we come to a sudden stop, they open the door.

'This is your stop miss.' I look out and see a hospital emergency entrance.

'Who are you?' I ask, and he grimaces and just says one thing.

'Shadow sends his regards.'

Holy crap. Shadow sent them to help me, not the general. He saved my life. He saved me from God knows what they were going to end up doing to me. The thought makes me shudder. I step out of the van and it drives away, the door closing behind me as they do. I mouth, 'Thank you', but I don't know if they saw it or not. I turn to stumble towards the entrance when an ambulance officer spots me and heads my way while shouting something at her co-worker.

She catches me just as I start to fall, 'What's your name? What happened to you?'

'My name is Samantha Erkhart. I was run off the road and taken hostage. Please call this number and inform them of my situation.' I hand her the card James gave me that first day we met, which I'd taken to carrying in my back pocket ever since. They lift me on to the stretcher and wheel me into the hospital. I drop in and out of consciousness a few times while they check me over before going out completely.

As I come too once more, I find myself in a hospital bed. I can see a nurse checking on me and guards on the door. They are our guys. James knows now what is going on. I relax at that. I am safe. For now.

UNEXPECTED ALLY

⊡

I LOOK AROUND the hospital room again as I stir. The guards are still on the door. No nurse this time fussing over me, but I see James outside just past the guards talking to someone on my team. They don't look happy at all. I guess it is not over, whatever is happening. James sees me watching him, he says something to whoever he is talking to and turns towards me. He comes past the guards and closes the door behind him.

'I know I told you to do whatever it took to catch him, to get me the bad guy, but did you have to go and do all of that?' I don't say anything. Honestly, I am not sure which parts he knows about, I wouldn't want to make my situation worse. Maybe it is best to just hear what I am in trouble for first and leave the rest out of the conversation for now.

'You know how to have a good time, don't you? You go on a hacking spree halfway around the world, you turn the power off for half of Brisbane and you almost go and get yourself killed by some completely crazy international crime syndicate which you had pissed off in some of your previous life adventures.'

I nod, 'that sounds about right to me.'

I wait patiently for James to continue. He just looks at me for a few moments before deciding to continue. 'But do you know what surprises me the most, you got your target to somehow enlist a criminal hit squad, one of the best in the world to go in and take out half the syndicate thugs, snatch you up just before they did monstrous things to you and then just drop you off at the hospital.' Wow, he is right, that is pretty out there.

'Honestly, Sir—'

He gives me a bit of a look, 'Don't you think we are way past Sir by now Sam?'

I nod. '—James, I don't know anything about why Shadow helped me. I don't know anything about the hit squad except that they are the most lethal strike team I have ever seen. I have never seen anything like them in my life. They took out those people like they were nothing.

I didn't call for help or even ask for it. Shadow, for a reason I am not certain of yet, took it on himself to save me.' I fiddle with the starched hospital sheet. 'I honestly don't know why but I am very grateful that I did not need to endure what I know was coming to me. My torturer had already informed me of what it was they were going to be doing to me. I'm very happy I did not need to endure such events. I barely made it through the ones he was able to do to me before they arrived.'

James nodded 'I am certain you are right, what Shadow's angle is though is not certain. Maybe you have in some way bonded with him, maybe he enjoys your interactions, your game of cat and mouse. Maybe he just didn't want to see that happen to you. Maybe it helped him claim more power and you were just part of a wider scheme. I am not sure we will ever know his true intentions.'

'He contacted us, you know. Told us you were here and that you needed protection. He has given us everything we need to take the cartel down. We have everything about them and our teams are moving on their sites as we speak. This is going to be a good win for our team, likely a promotion for you and me keeping my job, which I am quite happy about. It was looking very bad for me over the last couple of weeks, but they can't get rid of the general who brought down the world's biggest cartel, now can they?'

I blink. 'What about Shadow?' he smiles at that question.

'For now Sam, I think he can have a head start on us, we can wait till you are feeling better and then maybe you can help track him down again. Does that sound reasonable to you? I think he has earned that much from us, don't you think?' I nod in agreement.

'I don't know how much you remember, but you made a mess of your car. It is a complete mess but you don't need to worry, we will fix it or get you the new model if we can't. Maybe this time we could get you a few upgrades in body armour and performance, it sure seems like you could probably use it. What do you think?' I have a smile now ear to ear. 'I will take that as a yes shall I Sam.' He turns towards the door. 'Get some rest, Sam, we will need your skills back as soon as you are capable. The bad guys don't rest you know' I just nod. He turns and leaves the room. I see him talking to the guards before he leaves.

I can't believe that Shadow is the reason I am still here in one piece. Why did he do it? Why is he on my side? I was trying to put him in jail but he saved me. I hope that is the last I will see of the cartel, though. Another shudder runs through my body at the thought of that monster I almost got a little too acquainted with. The idea still completely terrifies me. I don't think I will be sleeping well for a little while, I have enough to keep me waking in the middle of the night with cold sweats for years to come.

Enjoy our alliance, Shadow. It is not going to last long. Time to get some rest and get ready for round two. I think I may have lost this round but we are not done yet.

DOWNTIME

IT'S BEEN NEARLY a week since I was taken hostage and rescued by Shadow's team. I honestly looked like I went 10 rounds with Mike Tyson with all the bruises I had all over my body. I don't know if they are from the crash or my abductors, but it's almost easier to find the patches of skin that aren't bruised than count all the bruises. Dad hasn't been at work much this week, he hovers around me, making sure I have everything I need.

I got a surprise yesterday with the delivery of over 1000 roses, from Shadow, of course. He included a card, embossed with an angel that you could feel if you run your finger over the paper, It read: *I hope you have a quick recovery. I'm looking forward to continuing our game*. I still don't know why he saved me, but Dad wanted to know who was sending me all of these roses. I still haven't explained.

I said I couldn't talk about it yet as I wasn't sure what was happening myself. It is true, I don't know what is going on, does he like me, is that it? Does he just love the game of cat and mouse because I can challenge him? I could be better than him. If he's anything like me, it's the challenge of our dynamic; we make things more interesting for each other.

I am going to have to ask Shadow why he saved me when I talk to him. I will talk to him again, the flowers make that pretty clear.

I cringe as I get out of bed, aggravating my shoulder. It is good to be home, the last week at the hospital was starting to get on my nerves. I look out the window and still see the protective detail on our house. James thinks Shadow or one of the cartel stragglers they haven't captured yet could try to get to me. He wants to be prepared either way. I agree with him, especially after the whole abduction situation. Shadow, on the other hand, isn't likely to come here. He's smarter than that but even if he did, I don't think he would want to hurt me.

Although Dad might, he is a over the two pallets of toilet paper in our lounge room. I have to admit it is a little funny and I would probably laugh if I wasn't the one who had paid for it all. I will need to find some way of returning all of it or get it put in storage somewhere else, if not. Maybe I could sell it to the kids who'd been in the year below me, for their end-of-year muck up day. Every year it seems to be a staple item for them to throw around everywhere, would be a good way to get it out of the house.

I head into the bathroom. I need to have a shower, try and loosen these aching muscles. I close the door and unbutton my shirt. I carefully slide off my underwear and unclip my bra, it hurts much more than I would like to admit. I flick my clothes over to the dirty laundry basket in the corner and turn toward the shower when I catch a glimpse of myself in the mirror.

My bruising has gone all green and yellow. My whole body almost looks like I am wearing some sort of faded camo gear. A random pattern of yellows, greens, blacks and white. It looks interesting and if it wasn't so painful, I might find it amusing. I am lucky to be alive if I am honest with myself. I need to be more careful, maybe even learn to look after myself better. James has already discussed me doing some advanced combat training when I return to work. I am not looking forward to that, but I know it's necessary. I need to be prepared for the next time something like this occurs.

I stand in the shower for a long time, soaking up the heat and breathing in the steam. I do feel much better. I get out and put on some comfortable clothes. There's no one around to see me except Dad so it doesn't matter how I look.

I slowly make my way downstairs wincing at each step, Dad hears me and rushes to help but I wave him off.

'I need to start doing things for myself again. I'm not a cripple.' He gives me a scowling look before just doing it anyway. We get halfway down the stairs when he turns to me.

'You have a visitor. He is one of your team, I was going to turn him away, but then I heard you coming down the stairs, so I invited him in.' that's strange why would one of my team to see me? Maybe its Gabby. I look out the window and the SUV is gone. Maybe they have caught all of the cartel. Maybe I am safe again. I breathe a little easier at that thought than I realise what I am wearing, probably the most embarrassing clothes I own. Track pants, tucked into thick cosy socks and the daggiest shirt. Great. Brilliant decision Sam. Oh well. Whoever it is will need to just deal with it.

We get to the bottom of the stairs and Dad gestures towards the lounge room. He's waiting for you in there. 'Do you want me to get you something to eat and drink?'

I nod, leaning slightly against the wall to catch my breath. 'I'll find out what they want and get rid of them.' He smiles and turns towards the kitchen. I make my way towards the lounge room, and whoever my guest is. I stop completely in my tracks.

'Good morning Sam. You look like you are improving.' It's Shadow, sitting in my lounge room. He is sitting over to one side in my dad favourite chair, the only recliner we have. 'I wanted to check on you before I move on, make sure you were recovering well and it looks like you are.' What should I do? Holy crap, what do I say to Dad? What is he doing here? Shadow looks into my eyes. 'I was very sorry all that happened to you. That is not something I would like you to have experienced. I didn't see them coming, I am sorry for that.'

What, why does he care? Why should he have seen them coming?

'Why are you here? Why did you save me?' he softens a little in his appearance, with a slight smile touching his lips.

'I am here to see you, silly.' He takes a step closer. 'You already know why I saved you, I like you Sam and I think you like me too?' That statement angers me. The ego on him is ridiculous. How could he think I like him? He's my target that's it.

Isn't it...?

Yes, he's my target; the mission I've been assigned. A *job*. That's all he is. I am not calling for backup right now because he saved my life, nothing else. I owe him that, at least. 'Don't be ridiculous, I don't like you like that. I am going to arrest you. Not today. I owe you that at least. But I will find you again and I will arrest you.' He smiles and takes another step towards me. He is very close to me now, close enough to touch me, kiss me even, there are only centimetres between us, I can almost feel his heat on my body.

'What are you doing?' I whisper. He smiles at me and inches closer still. I like his close proximity more than I want to admit, I like how it make me feel alive, the fact he is close enough to touch me. I know it's wrong, I know I need to put a stop to this now.

'I wanted to make sure you were safe. Your team is busy with the last of the intel I sent through to them. They will have the remaining members of the cartel in minutes if they don't mess it up.'

'I can't stay long. I just wanted to say goodbye. I am looking forward to our next game of skill.' He is crazy, he is flirting with me. He likes me, like, really likes me. No, that can't be right. It doesn't matter anyway, I don't date criminals, especially ones I am hunting. We hold each other's gaze for what feels like a minute before he leans forward and kisses me. I feel his lips on mine, a soft caress. I don't resist even though I know I should. Stop, stop, stop Sam. You can't do this; he is your target. I pull back and push him back away from me slightly. He doesn't resist.

He touches his mouth and smiles, 'Goodbye Sam.' I don't respond. I am still in shock about what just happened. I watch him walk through the front door and disappear. What the hell was that? Oh, this just got even messier. Great one, Sam. Just great.

I push that all out of my mind and stomp toward the kitchen. I can't deal with whatever that was just now. Breakfast with Dad is what I need, another distraction, that's what I need.

That's the last I saw of Shadow, although not the last time I thought of him. It's that kiss, the soft exhilarating kiss that both excites me and pisses me off in the same thought. My thoughts are clouded with emotion that I can't get under control. I need to push it all away though. I need to focus. I can't let myself fall for him. I just can't.

BACK TO WORK

IT'S BEEN A FEW weeks since the accident. All the bruising has cleared up and I feel really good. Today it is time to go back to work. I am so over being at home; I need to get out of here and get back to what I do best. James was right when he said his job would be safe and I would probably end up with a promotion. The agency loved what we did with the cartel, they ignored all of the other mess and just took the positive they got from the top. Brining down a huge syndicate was massive. So, although I am not sure I am qualified but I am now the permanent team leader for my team, I don't know how they will take me being their new boss but I guess we will have to make it work. They all still know a lot more about their world than I do so I will lean on them for that but when it comes to the cyber world, none of them can even come close to me and they all know that now.

The recent escapade has done one thing for me at least and that is garner some respect from the team. Hopefully, the promotion doesn't ruin any of that for me. I finish getting dressed, I look in the mirror and almost don't recognise myself. I am not a kid anymore; I am a woman. From my sharp suit and the serious expression on my face, I look like I was born for this gig. I look amazing. A strong woman, ready to command my team.

Why wasn't I wearing something like this when Shadow turned up in my lounge room? I had to be wearing sweat pants and a sweatshirt that looks like it was fit for the rag bin. I shouldn't care, what he thinks but I do, it is driving me crazy. I will not let it get the better of me though, I will find him and capture him. He means nothing more to me than a target. Never mind that he saved my life… and that he kisses really well. He's just a target.

Keep telling yourself that Sam. How can I deny it, even just to myself that I don't have any feelings for him, I know there is something there, there shouldn't be but there still is nonetheless. He challenges me intellectually and when he kissed me there is no denying the chemistry between us. He doesn't mean anything to me. Maybe if I say it enough I might actually start to believe it…

I shake off the thought of him, focus Sam. I pick up my bag and head downstairs my ride will be here soon. I need to have breakfast with Dad, he is already very nervous about me going back to work, he is scared that I won't be so lucky next time, I kinda agree with him. Not that I will admit that.

Breakfast goes by quickly, we chat and laugh and just enjoy each other's company. It's good to be able to do this again, it has been a bit different since I got hurt but this gives me hope. Things might go back to normal around here. I get a ding on my phone; the car is arriving. I start to get up when Dad puts his arms around me 'Be safe okay.' I just nod 'You look great, go knock 'em dead.'

I walk out to the SUV; it's waiting for me in front of our house. Jake is my driver today, it's great to see a familiar face. He opens the door for me as I get closer.

Jake smiles and closes the door behind me once I am safely in the car.

'It's good to have you back with us.' I look at him in the eyes in the revision mirror, as I did months earlier.

'It's good to be back.' I truly mean that. I've had enough of all this laying around, getting better. The fussing and the pampering. Honestly, it was good to start with but there is only so much a girl like me can take. Enough is enough. I want to get back into my world, the one I have strong control in, the one I am my true self. Foresight.

I know things will be different now. I am not the unknown outsider; I am now one of them. One who probably scares them a little. I'll embrace my new position, I will push its boundaries and I will make sure that I leave my mark on this place. Good or bad, it will be permanent, like a stain you can't get out of your carpet.

As we make the usual drive to the office, I look out the window. Everything feels as though it is moving at a slower pace outside like everything is almost in slow motion. It's a weird feeling. The people going about their daily lives, none of them knows what is going on around them, what battles are being waged for them. They will likely never know and that's the way the powers that be like it. I don't know if it's right, but that's the world we live in, one which I am now a big part of. What we do is worth it. We save so many lives but you will never see us on the news, you will never see me in a newspaper. It wouldn't be allowed to happen. We round the corner near the office. I am nearly there.

My phone springs to life, it's a message from Shadow: *Enjoy your first day back*. It's the first time I have heard from him since the kiss. I just stare at his message, I don't respond. He must be keeping tabs on me.

When I walk into the office and make my way towards my desk, everyone in the room starts clapping and cheering.

Gabby walks up to me, 'Welcome back boss.' Boss. Wow, I think I could get used to that. When the commotion settles down, she continues, 'We have a briefing in the General's office in five minutes. You won't be getting time to settle back in we have a new target to find.'

'What about Shadow, has he dropped down in priority?' I ask. I'd kind of counted on having everyone's backing to find him again.

'Shadow has been feeding us intel on some of the worst of the worst.' Gabby says, looking like she has complicated feelings about it. So, Shadow is continuing to help the agency. Is it because of me? Does he want to get close to me or is he just using us to do his dirty work? I am going to have to find out. Gabby hooks her elbow through mine, towing me down the hall. 'Let's go, Boss, we don't want to keep the General waiting. You might be in the good books now, but the way you do things, I am sure that tide will change in no time.' She digs me in the ribs with that statement. Gabby and I are going to be great friends I can just see it already.

Time to get to work…

SMACKDOWN

⧉

SWEAT IS DRIPPING DOWN my face, it beads all over my body. I am sore and beaten. I am lying face down on the mat with an overgrown hairy ape on my back. Seriously, man, you need to do some personal grooming. This is getting ridiculous. He looks like he hasn't shaved in years. I try to twist and move to get out of his grip. I am getting good at this whole hand to hand combat stuff but he has got me pinned well. I pause as they have taught me, study your situation, figure out your move, then commit to it. Put everything you have into it; it could be what saves your life.

I lay still, considering my options.

'Tap out Sam, you have nowhere to go.' He could be right, but I am stubborn and hate to lose. I think I could get my leg up high enough to swing it over his shoulder. If I can do that, I could push him over and manoeuver into a strong position, one I could pin him with. My legs are my strongest asset apart from my mind. I use them both to my advantage, many underestimate me. I am small and I know it. They don't see me as a threat and it gives me plenty of opportunities to use that against them.

I swing my leg around, hooking my knee around his throat. He realises what I am about to do and tries to dodge, but It's too late. I pull back hard on my leg, twisting my hips sharply as I do, spinning him backwards underneath me. Securing him in place under my unrelenting grip between my legs, my thigh and calf cutting off the blood flow to his head. He is getting bright red, struggling against my grip but the more he moves, the tighter I hold on, like a python strangling its prey.

He isn't tapping out though; he's stubborn, just like me. A few more moments and it won't matter he will be napping on the mat. I hold until I see him lose conciseness. He is going to have a headache when he wakes up, I know, I have passed out a few times myself through all this training. He goes limp and that's my cue. I release him from my hold and climb off the ape.

I stand back, looking at him lying there enjoying a well-deserved rest. He looks peaceful almost. One of the other guys sticks something under his nose and he jolts back to the real world.

'Nap is over, big guy. Time to get back to reality.' He rolls over to his knees, slowly, I assume he is still affected and a little foggy about what just happened. He got beaten by a girl, something many of the guys I have been training with of late have had to come to grips with. I have found a talent I didn't even know I had. Adaptability in battle is probably a big part of it though. I can adjust, shift, change focus as needed. My path is never concrete.

He shakes off the fogginess and gets to his feet. He walks across the mat and stands right in front of me, I have to crane my neck to look up at him.

'Nice job Sam. You did it again. You kicked my ass all over this mat. Maybe sometime you could let me win? It would help with my bruised ego.' I smile at him, but I will never let them win, ever. That's not my style.

'If you beat me, it will be because you have done so for real. I don't have it in me to throw a fight. You know that.'

He likes my response. 'Sam, I don't know if I will ever beat you, but I can keep trying.' He puts out his hand for me to shake, I take it and he pulls me in for a sort of bear hug. It's a little gross, he is very sweaty and hairy. No boundaries in this place. When he finally lets me down, I turn to grab my stuff and go hit the showers. Time for play is over, back to the real work.

I have been doing a lot of this training since I returned to work, weapons training, hand to hand combat. Every day, no rain-checks. I am getting stronger physically and mentally every time and I haven't lost at combat for weeks. I have some work to do with gun accuracy, but I am above average for the team. Which is good considering I have never held a gun before a few weeks ago. The rest of the team have been honing their skills for years now. Many are ex-military, police or shadow organisations that are a little hard to classify especially as no one talks about it, ever. I don't mind all the secrecy. It lets me keep to myself. I have never been a big oversharer, so this place fits me well.

GAME ON

IT'S BEEN A FEW WEEKS since I started back at work. We've taken down three targets. None of them have the skills of Shadow, or me, for that matter. Script kiddies, wannabes. They aren't much of a challenge to the team at all. I have been letting them do the footwork, teaching them some tricks, why they are working. The team is meshing very well and have embraced me as the team lead. They don't question anything I ask them to do, they just respond and get it done.

Everything is just going along smoothly, so much so that I am waiting for the other shoe to drop. You know when everything is going great, things are just happening and then it happens. Something really horrible or just painful happens and you're screwed. That's what I am waiting for. For the chips to fall as they may and for chaos to ensue.

Today could be one of those moments when everything

falls apart. We are prepping for a surveillance op, we will be watching a handoff of stolen intel. There is a meeting set at 11 in Anzac square. The teams are getting into place, blending into the environment. I will be watching from across the square. Now that I have completed my advanced combat training, which I totally aced, of course, I am allowed to go on ops like these. I even carry a gun some days. Not today though, it could give us away if it was spotted during the op.

We make our way to the location of the exchange and I get in position. I have a clear line of sight to the target area. I am just sitting surfing the web on my phone like almost every other person around.

We have some time before our targets are set to arrive. We needed to be in position. I have already been here for almost an hour. Others in the team come and go like normal people just going about their business. It is pretty interesting to watch when you know who they are and how they blend in, doing mostly nothing extraordinary. Occasionally, some will draw slight attention to themselves by doing something a bit out there. Almost hiding in plain sight, but without trying to hide at all.

They are good. If I didn't know who they are, I don't think I would pick them out even when I am looking for them. We really do have a skilled and experienced team. I wonder how many times they have done something like this. It would have to be thousands, hundreds of times. I don't think any of them would tell me if I asked, but it would be an interesting fact to know. I wonder how much time it took them to perfect the art of hiding in plain sight. I am still mastering it myself, I am getting better, but I always feel a little weird and out of place.

I don't know if that is the situation or just me in general

though. I have always felt out of place as Sam, Foresight has always been my comfort zone. I think it probably always will, even as I build confidence as Sam. I glance around, it must be getting close to hand off now. Time to focus, get another capture under our team's belt. If we keep this up we will get a reputation in our circles, maybe even a few more promotions for the team and maybe myself.

I watch as the first of our targets arrive. They look a little nervous. He is fidgety and keeps looking around, watching everyone to see if they are watching him. It makes sense, they are selling government secrets to a foreign entity. I would be nervous about it too if it were me. That's a get shoved into a black hole, never to see the light of day kind of crime. I hope they are getting paid very well for this, I hope whatever the reward is it is all worth the risk. They are going to find out very soon the consequences.

They look around and make their way over to the designated meeting place. They settle in on a bench not much different from the one I am currently sitting on. You know, those park seats with a concrete frame and timber slats spread across them. They are very uncomfortable after more than 20 minutes or so. I wonder if it is deliberate to stop people sitting on them too long or is it just about durability.

Focus Sam. Focus on the task at hand. Their contact arrives. They look calm and collected. They are a professional, this isn't their first time. They scan the area around them looking for anything out of the ordinary. They take a seat on the opposite side of the area, not doing much, just surveying the movement of the public space. Just analysing, learning the patterns, looking for any abnormalities. After about 20 minutes of this, they seem to be happy with what they see. Nothing seems to jump out at them and they decide to continue with the exchange.

They approach the target, still watching checking for anything off. As they near their contact they slow down and pause for a few moments longer before making their move. It is over in a split second; they say a few words as they exchange but I can't make out what it was. They turn away from each other and start to head off in separate ways.

The exchange is complete and we have a go. We will take down both parties, but we want to follow them for a while first to see what else we can glean from this situation. We might be able to find out who the bosses of this exchange are, what they want and why.

I will be casually following our first target, the one who just sold the secrets. He is less a priority as we already know everything about him, where he lives, who he works for and even what he has for breakfast most days. The rest of the team will follow our professional in rotations so he doesn't figure out he is being followed. My guy is not very good at that, so he won't even know I am here. Perfect training for me, a way to hone my skills and become one with the surroundings. Part of the furniture, so to speak, not something I am very good at yet but it is all about the practice, I guess.

I wait for the other team to do their thing before casually getting to my feet and heading off in the direction of my target. I see him up ahead walking quickly down the street about 50 meters in front of me. I seem to follow him slowly through the city for what feels like an hour, he is doing circles. I think he is trying to be clever and lose a tail if he had one, maybe he is a little paranoid. I don't blame him, I guess what he is doing is risky. I would like to know if it is just greed or if he has a higher calling or cause that he feels he is fulfilling with this.

I think we must be on our 10th lap now. I know I've passed

this place at least that many times now. He walks across a pedestrian crossing over to the other side of the road. I continue to stroll down the same side of the road, keeping him in my sights and head towards the next crossing ahead. I don't think I will lose him. He has been doing the same path over and over. I have some time and space to just let him feel safe, to just relax and head back to work. His office is just around the corner and I think he is going back this time, but I have thought that a couple of times. He gets right outside and just diverts away at the last minute.

I walk up to the edge of the crossing and just as I am stepping out, a car screeches to a halt in front of me. I jump back a few feet and resist the urge to curse. It's a dark blue tesla sport with windows completely darkened; I can't see the driver. I wait for it to move but it doesn't. Others walk around it on the crossing and just continue with their day. My phone vibrates in my pocket. I take it out and see a message: *Get in.* It's Shadow, what does he want? I look past the car to try and find my target but he is gone. My phone vibrates again: *Get in the car Sam.*

I huff and just decide to go with it. This better not be a trap or so help me, I will make his life very miserable. I reach for the back door handle and climb in. No one else is in the back seat. I slide on in and pull the door closed. As soon as I do, it starts to drive. I look over at the driver's seat, it's empty. What the hell is going on? I might have made a big mistake getting in here.

I look around the car, analysing my situation. Nothing looks out of the ordinary, apart from the fact the car is driving all by itself. It's a tesla version of Kit, you know the car in those old knight rider shows. It looks like Shadow has figured out how to do it, manipulate the autopilot function, let the car do the driving solo. Apart from this being a bit weird, it's not that big of a leap from the car's normal capabilities. They really can handle almost anything thrown at them, probably better than humans can. Faster response, better decisions in bad situations.

It's the way of the future, if we like it or not. Humans will become obsolete in the transport arena. It will be interesting to see if it's passenger drones or autonomous vehicles that will be our future or if it will be a bit of both. I think it will be both and I think I am enjoying my chauffeured ride, even if I would have preferred to know where I am going and what the hell I am doing in this bloody car. A real-life kit, it is pretty cool. I wish he had gone with a mustang. I love them and I thought the series remake was pretty sweet. Maybe I could build my own sometime or get Telsa to put me one together. I am sure they could make it happen. It might cost me a pretty penny, though definitely worth every cent.

The car drives out of the city and down some back streets for about 20 minutes or so more. Where are we going? I am starting to get a little concerned that getting in this car may have been a really stupid idea. Shadow is a criminal, yes he has been helping my team get some great wins, but he is a criminal when it all boils down. I can't trust him, I don't know him well enough and I have no idea of what his true motives are for helping the team or me in general.

I know I keep letting that kiss cloud my judgement, I should know better than to let a school girl crush on the bad boy put me in harm's way like this. James and my team are going to be unhappy I just jumped in this car without having an end game or a way to get back up when I need it. I realise that I still have my phone and my team is tracking me. It was part of the op, a way to keep track of the target and record his movement. I reach down and pull the phone from my pocket. The signal is out. I should have known better than to think he wouldn't have already thought of that.

This is Shadow I am dealing with, after all. He is a master planner, always one step ahead of us, maneuvering pieces into place before we even considered them at all. He might be second best to me with cyber skills, but I have nothing on him when it comes to strategy. I have always thought of myself as good at the game of chess, manipulating situations to my advantage, but he has pure skill. One I will admit I admire a little. I would never tell him that though, his ego would probably get too much of a kick out of that.

The car comes to a stop at a set of traffic lights and I consider getting out of the car. I shouldn't be in here. I reach for the door handle when suddenly Shadow enters the car from the other side, sliding in next to me. As he pulls his door closed, the car takes off again at a much higher speed than before. He must be worried about being followed.

'Tesla one, change colour to grey, avoid surveillance zones.' What? A car can't just change its colour like that or even drive itself like this, avoiding surveillance. I look at the bonnet of the car through the windscreen and I can't believe what I am seeing. It starts to change into a dark grey almost gunmetal look. What the hell? That isn't possible, is it?

Is this how he escaped our trap in the Porsche? Was it driving on its own and we didn't even know or was this car waiting for him to do a changeover? Smooth, silent and almost untraceable. I think I may have underestimated my opponent, again. I really should stop doing that.

He looks over at me.

'I missed you Sam. You look good.' I don't respond just

hold his gaze. He holds it for a few moments, long enough for it to get a bit personal, making me want to avert my gaze but I hold it.

'So what is this all about? What do you want?' He looks a bit uncomfortable with that question, like he doesn't want to answer.

I see him take a deep breath.

'I need your help...'

ABOUT THE AUTHOR

CRAIG FORD is a cybersecurity engineer and ethical hacker. He has a Masters of Management (Information Technology) and a Masters of Information Systems Security from Charles Sturt University. He was awarded the AISA (Australian Information Security Association) Cyber security professional of the year 2020 and was elected AISA Brisbane branch Chair in 2021. Craig is a freelance cybersecurity Journalist who is best known for his work on CSO Australia in which he contributed almost 100 cybersecurity articles between 2018-2020. He is a regular columnist for "Women in Security" Magazine and has contributed to the project since its inception in early 2021. Craig has two previous books "A Hacker, I Am" and "A Hacker, I Am – Vol 2" which were self-published, these are cybersecurity awareness books which try and help educate everyone on how to be safer in this connected world.

Shawline Publishing Group Pty Ltd

www.shawlinepublishing.com.au